M000279661

He silenced her with a kiss

Kate seemed surprised, but it was inevitable to William. Her lips were soft and warm. He held her closer; she twined her arms around his neck. She tasted of chocolate, sweet and mysterious.

"All day," he breathed, lifting his mouth a fraction from hers, "all day I've wanted to do this."

Kate attempted to straighten her dress. "Another international experience no one will believe."

"Why not?"

"I'm not exactly the type who makes men crazy with lust."

"You're not?" She could have fooled *him*.

Kate smiled. She thought he was joking, he realized.

"It's the dress, then," he declared, keeping his voice light. Her coat was open to reveal the amber beads draped over that tempting cleavage. Kate shifted and the yellow stone on her lapel blinked and winked at him. He closed his eyes briefly, trying to remember what he was supposed to be doing. The brooch.

He was only after her because of the brooch. He had to remember that....

London, England, is a very romantic place according to **Kristine Rolofson.** This multitalented author toured the city with a girlfriend researching *Make-Believe Honeymoon.* The trip was a gift from her husband—and a break away from being a busy mother of six! The glamour and romance of the city convinced Kristine she had to return with her husband. She and her husband did just that in celebrating their twenty-fifth wedding anniversary.

Books by Kristine Rolofson

HARLEQUIN TEMPTATION
425—THE PERFECT HUSBAND
469—I'LL BE SEEING YOU
478—MADELEINE'S COWBOY
494—BABY BLUES
507—PLAIN JANE'S MAN
548—JESSIE'S LAWMAN

Don't miss any of our special offers. Write to us at the following address for information on our newest releases.

Harlequin Reader Service
U.S.: 3010 Walden Ave., P.O. Box 1325, Buffalo, NY 14269
Canadian: P.O. Box 609, Fort Erie, Ont. L2A 5X3

Kristine Rolofson
MAKE-BELIEVE HONEYMOON

Harlequin Books

TORONTO • NEW YORK • LONDON
AMSTERDAM • PARIS • SYDNEY • HAMBURG
STOCKHOLM • ATHENS • TOKYO • MILAN
MADRID • WARSAW • BUDAPEST • AUCKLAND

If you purchased this book without a cover you should be aware
that this book is stolen property. It was reported as "unsold and
destroyed" to the publisher, and neither the author nor the
publisher has received any payment for this "stripped book."

To Karen Venturini, first-class international babe and
London gift-shop connoisseur. I couldn't have done it
without you.

ISBN 0-373-25660-4

MAKE-BELIEVE HONEYMOON

Copyright © 1995 by Kristine Rolofson.

All rights reserved. Except for use in any review, the reproduction or
utilization of this work in whole or in part in any form by any electronic,
mechanical or other means, now known or hereafter invented, including
xerography, photocopying and recording, or in any information storage
or retrieval system, is forbidden without the written permission of the
publisher, Harlequin Enterprises Limited, 225 Duncan Mill Road,
Don Mills, Ontario, Canada M3B 3K9.

All characters in this book have no existence outside the imagination of
the author and have no relation whatsoever to anyone bearing the same
name or names. They are not even distantly inspired by any individual
known or unknown to the author, and all incidents are pure invention.

This edition published by arrangement with Harlequin Books S.A.

® and TM are trademarks of the publisher. Trademarks indicated with
® are registered in the United States Patent and Trademark Office, the
Canadian Trade Marks Office and in other countries.

Printed in U.S.A.

"YOU'RE PACKING an awful lot of black clothes." Anne frowned at the contents of the suitcase. "Are they some sort of symbol of your mood these days?"

Kate tossed another package of black panty hose into her new Pullman suitcase, bought on sale at JC Penney's the previous week. She'd packed and repacked her suitcase three times, caught between trying to be prepared for any weather and refusing to drag a suitcase that weighed more than she did. "The shoe salesman at Jordan Marsh told me that everyone in London wears black. If you wear sneakers and jeans and a windbreaker, you look like an American."

"So? You *are* an American."

"I want to look like I fit in," Kate explained. "I want to look sophisticated and worldly when I'm in England."

Her older sister snorted. "You're crazy. You could take the money and go someplace warm. Who goes to London in March?"

"I do. Especially now."

"Well, maybe it's a good idea that you get away from here," Anne conceded. "Who would have thought he'd find someone else and get married so fast?"

Both of them knew who "he" was. "I'm not angry." Kate considered a yellow sweater, then tossed it back onto the bed. "Breaking our engagement was very brave of him."

"*Brave?* He's a rat."

Kate winced. She was to have married Jeffrey Lannigan next week, then he'd announced at the last minute that he'd reconsidered. "I guess I don't have very good luck with men."

Anne nodded her agreement. "You're entirely too trusting. Remember that football player in high school? The one who dated three other girls while you thought you were going steady? And then in college, the chemistry major, wasn't it? Ray something? Didn't you pay for all your dates because he told you—"

"He had discovered the cure for cancer and needed all his money for research equipment," Kate said. "I'm going to change," she promised. She didn't want to be reminded of her past ... misunderstandings. Having three older sisters meant she had three people in her life who remembered every little mistake she'd ever made and weren't shy about pointing them out.

Anne smiled. "Not too much, I hope. We might not recognize you."

"I'm going to be very sophisticated and cool from now on. I'm through with men. When I get back from England, I'm going to buy a dog." She looked at her watch. "I have to hurry up and get out of here."

"A dog? What kind of dog?"

"Something small and friendly."

"I'll look into it for you," her sister said. "Carol might have some suggestions, too. You wouldn't want to buy the wrong—" She stopped as Kate tossed black tights into the suitcase. "More black? You'll look like you're going to a royal funeral."

"Hey, I'm feeling a little grim around the edges lately." Kate tossed in a pair of black flats and tried to divert Anne's attention from her wardrobe. "Maybe I'll get lucky and see the queen."

"Yeah, right." Anne shook her head. "And Di, too. Tell them both I said hello."

Kate folded a cream cardigan and placed it carefully in the suitcase. "You never know, Annie. You're joking, but I could see them somewhere. I'm going to have my camera ready all the time, especially when I go to Kensington Palace."

"A trip will take your mind off things, I suppose. You can look for a new job when you get back." Anne picked up a pair of black pants from the bed. "I thought you had your colors done and weren't supposed to wear black anymore."

"I did. I'm an 'autumn.' I'm supposed to wear browns and golds and cream colors. But so much of my stuff is black I have to bring a mix." Kate held up a pair of brown stretch pants. "Black and brown go together, right?"

"Very sophisticated," Anne agreed. "What about earrings?"

"I bought gold dangles with black and brown beads. And now I can wear Aunt Laurabelle's old pin. I always thought it had too much yellow in it." Kate took a large oval brooch from her dresser and tossed it to her sister. "I think it will look great on my coat, don't you?"

Anne held it up to the light. "It's quite, uh, big. I'm glad you ended up with it and not me."

"It was one of Aunt Belle's favorite pieces. She wore it on special occasions, don't you remember? She gave it to me before she died, said it would bring my heart's desire." Anne placed the pin in the V of Kate's new chestnut knit dress and nodded her approval. The large yellow rectangular stone in the center was surrounded by smaller white and green stones, in an interesting geometric design. "It looks good with the brown, too, doesn't it?" Kate asked.

"Yes, it does. Heart's desire, huh? Maybe you should have it appraised. What if it's valuable? You may need to have it insured."

Kate laughed. "The stones are too big to be anything but glass. But it supposedly came from England, so I'll wear it. For a good-luck charm."

"Why don't you wait until school gets out and I can go with you?"

"I've told you before. I have the reservations and I won't have any trouble. London's supposed to be a very safe city." She smiled at Anne's worried expression. Her other sisters had said the same thing. None of them believed she could exist without their help, which was ridiculous. They'd bossed her around for twenty-five years, but this time she wasn't listening. This time she was getting on a plane and doing something she wanted to do, without their advice and without their interference. "And everyone speaks English. Don't worry about me. I'll be fine by myself."

"I wish you were taking one of those organized tours instead of exploring all alone."

"I didn't want someone telling me how long I could take doing this or doing that. There are things I want to see that aren't offered on a tour. I want to walk around and explore and daydream about what it must have been like two hundred years ago. I'm going to eat fish and chips and drink beer."

"Well, be careful. Maybe you'll meet a sexy English-man in one of those pubs."

"I doubt it." Kate folded a black sweater and put it on the bed to consider. "I've heard they're very cold and reserved. And I'm not in the mood for flirting." Anne didn't really understand. How could she? She'd been married for four years and had an adorable two-year-old who wore pink bunny pajamas and kissed dolls. Kate winced. She'd dreamed of chubby babies and an adoring husband until Jeff had said, "I don't feel anything anymore." So much for the "adoring husband" fantasy.

"Dukes and lords and princes sound pretty interest-ing."

"I'll let you know when I get back." Kate smiled and picked up her aunt's brooch. *Heart's desire* was a little hard to believe. If she had what she wanted most, she'd be getting married next weekend. "I'd better put this on my coat now so I don't forget it."

Anne rolled her eyes. "I doubt if anyone could forget something that big and that gaudy."

Kate hesitated. "Do you think it's too much?"

"Not on black. Besides, it relieves that funereal look."

"All right." She pinned the brooch on the lapel of her wool coat and stood back to admire the affect. "I feel glamorous already."

"You look great," her sister agreed. "Especially with your hair that way. I'm glad you took Terri's advice and had it highlighted."

"Thanks." Kate's brown hair usually fell in a natural curl past her shoulders, but if she used the blow-dryer she could straighten it to look sleek and sophisticated.

It all depended on how much time she had in the morning, and today she'd taken her time. She wanted to look her best when she landed in England, even if it would be seven-thirty in the morning. After all, she still had her pride, or what was left of it after calling two hundred people to cancel her wedding. She zipped the suitcase shut.

Anne hopped off the bed. "Are you ready?"

Kate slung her coat over her arm and picked up the suitcase, which was still heavier than she would have liked. "Ready," she agreed. "From now on I'm an 'international babe.'"

Anne looked doubtful. "A 'babe,' huh?"

"Definitely." Kate grinned. "At least for the next ten days. I have it all figured out so I don't miss anything. Carol gave me a lot of brochures." She picked up three typed pages of activities and tucked them into her guidebook. She couldn't wait to leave Rhode Island. She couldn't bear to be around when Jeff married a woman he'd fallen in love with while buying socks at the mall, a woman he was marrying three weeks later.

Men were crazy, Kate decided. Men were crazy and unpredictable and bizarre. They told you one thing and did something else. They told you they loved you, then changed their minds. She'd buy that dog, Kate decided. A little fluffy dog that would curl up beside her on the couch and never, ever lie about love.

IT WASN'T RAINING, which made the afternoon quite comfortable, William Landry, the ninth Duke of Thornecrest observed. He looked upward, past the stone buildings and chimneys to the clouds scattered across the pale blue sky. Some of his friends were skiing in Gstaad; he could join them if the mood took him. Afterward he'd return to Thorne Hall in time for the spring planting.

There were always important things to do at home, he mused. Unlike London. He'd ordered new clothes at Turnbull & Asser, then he'd inspected a replacement chair for the dining room and, at Christie's, he'd listened to Gaylord rattle on about paintings and armoires for over an hour. He'd been in town for over a week, and tomorrow he could leave. He would have left already if Pitty hadn't kept coming up with excuses to keep him with her. For some reason she thought he'd find a wife in town this year. For some reason she thought he wanted one.

She couldn't be more mistaken.

He would now check in with his grandmother, describe every piece of Georgian furniture Gaylord had gushed over, change into appropriate clothes, then head to Wilton's for a long lunch with Lady Jessica Wilton, a tall silvery blonde who'd accepted the fact that he would never marry—at least not in this century.

William slowed down as he entered Essex Court, an exclusive London cul-de-sac. The bustling sounds of the city disappeared, left behind on St. James Street. On either side of Thorne House stood smaller town houses with the shining brass nameplates on immaculate white-painted doors their only introduction to the passerby.

A young woman stood on the front steps of Thorne House. An American, he guessed, noting the camera bag around her shoulder and the bright red *Guide to London* tucked under her arm. A tourist, of course, although they weren't as plentiful in March as they were in July, thank goodness. He'd been against showing the house, against making a deal with the Victoria and Albert Museum to allow tourists to traipse through the lower floors of the family's town house. But Pitty had insisted, and he'd acquiesced. As usual.

He stepped closer, unable to avoid the woman since she blocked his way to the front door. "Excuse me," he said, trying to be as polite as possible. "Is there something you need at Thorne House?"

"It's closed." She turned amazingly green eyes on him. Brown hair with gold-and-red highlights hung past the shoulders of her black coat. She swept her hair from her cheek, revealing a bright pin on the lapel of her coat. The yellow center stone winked and glowed in the weak sunlight. "I can't believe Thorne House is really closed," she repeated.

"You can't?" He lifted his gaze to her extremely pretty face and gave her a long look. She didn't come up to his chin. William backed up a step. He had no time for short American tourists, however attractive.

She shot another disappointed look at the brass plaque with Closed engraved upon it. "No. It's one of the places I most wanted to see. My great-aunt told me—"

"It's closed in the winter," he interrupted. "For refurbishment."

"That's a shame. I came all the way from Rhode Island—that's in America—to see this house." She turned back to the door, as if willing it to open by itself and allow her entrance.

He knew Rhode Island was in America. He'd even been there one summer, but he didn't particularly want to start a conversation with a stranger about his travels in the States. "It happens every year."

"What?"

"Refurbishment." He stuck his hands in the pockets of his worn leather jacket. "From January through March, you see."

"It didn't say anything about that in the guidebook."

"I'm awfully sorry." He waited for her to move away. It would seem cruel to pull out the key and step inside, leaving the young woman to stare up at the house, so he waited. She'd probably expect a private tour if she knew he lived in the house she'd come "all the way from Rhode Island" to visit. He wouldn't want to be rude; he merely wanted to go inside and change his clothes.

"Yes, so am I." She sighed and finally moved away from the door. "Are you touring London, too?"

William hid his amusement at being mistaken for a tourist. He knew he looked scruffy; he usually didn't wear blue jeans in the city. "In a way." She seemed to be waiting for him to explain. "I work in London occasionally," he said, which was not exactly a lie. He'd been working his ass off since he'd arrived last week. "And I particularly enjoy English history."

"Oh. You should understand, then."

"Yes," he agreed. "But there are other houses to see," he added, hoping to alleviate her obvious disappointment. "Somerset House is an art museum now, but the building is quite impressive, and so are the Impressionist collections. And Marlborough House is often open by appointment. It's around the corner."

The little American held up her guidebook and smiled. "Yes, I know."

"Have that book memorized, do you?"

"A little." She backed up a step, as if finally realizing she was standing in a foreign city talking to a strange man. "Well, thanks a lot for the information."

"My pleasure." He inclined his head in a small bow. "I hope you enjoy your vacation, despite this, er, disappointment."

"I will." She chuckled. "Unless you tell me that the Tower of London is closed for refurbishment, too."

"I wouldn't think of disappointing you."

She smiled a bit ruefully and turned to walk out of the courtyard. He waited for her to disappear onto St. James Street before he unlocked the entrance. The great hall was draped in white sheets, and the smell of paint hung thick in the air. He took the elevator to the third floor, where Pitty stood in the window, her binoculars around her neck. Her large face was flushed, her over-size bosom heaving with excitement.

"William! This is absolutely incredible! Who is she? Why didn't you ask her in?"

"Who are you spying on now?" He began to unbutton his jacket, anticipating a hot shower and a pleasant lunch.

"You, dear boy. Who was that woman?"

"A tourist."

"A *tourist?* Well, bring her back. I thought you knew her! Didn't you see me waving?"

"I wasn't looking at the windows. And how would I know an American tourist?" He joined her at the window and looked down at the empty court. "Good, she's gone. She was disappointed that she couldn't see inside the house. I thought for a moment she would refuse to leave."

She pointed to him and ordered, "Bring her back!"

"Pitty, your blood pressure—"

"Did you *see* it? Did you *see* what she *wore?*"

He frowned, trying to remember. "A coat, Pitty. A black coat, like every other woman in London." William began to worry. He could call her physician and have him here within minutes. Pitty was at least eighty, though she wouldn't reveal her age to anyone, not even the queen.

She pointed a finger at him. "The brooch. Didn't you notice the brooch?" Her hands fluttered over her chest. "The Thorne Diamond has returned at last! I never thought I'd live to see the day, but it has returned. Just in time, too, for I'm growing older, you know."

The Thorne Diamond, a six-carat canary-colored stone from the Kappur mine of India, was one of Pitty's favorite topics, usually discussed at the same time Pitty brought the subject of marriage to his attention. Although the diamond had disappeared two hundred years ago, he'd been forced to believe the jewel existed. After all, a painting in his home showed a Thornecrest duchess wearing the pin, but he couldn't imagine that it was the same jewel that twinkled from the shoulder of a stranger's coat, no matter what his grandmother thought. William went to the phone. "I'm going to call Dr. Halston and have him come over and pay a little visit...."

Pitty quivered with indignation. "You'll do no such thing. You'll find that woman and bring her back here, and she will tell me how the stone came into her possession! Go!"

He hesitated before picking up the receiver. "Why would a tourist possess such a priceless gem? And why would she wear it on her coat, as if it was a trinket?"

"That's exactly what I want you to discover, my boy. Now, go! Before she disappears."

William figured the attractive little American had had plenty of time to disappear, but he didn't want to add to his grandmother's anxiety. "I will if you promise to lie down while I'm gone. You shouldn't become so upset."

Pitty took him by the shoulders and pushed him toward the entry. "Go, Willie, please. I know I'm not mistaken. Bring her back her so I can purchase it."

"I shall do my best," William promised, heading toward the elevator. "If Jessica rings before I return, explain to her I'll be late, will you?"

Pitty clapped her hands. "Of course. This is perfect! Such a *lovely* girl, isn't she?"

William didn't bother answering; he'd become inured to his grandmother's attempts at matchmaking. To please her he would try to find the young woman, but the oddness of the situation struck him as humorous. The Duke of Thornecrest trailing a tourist . . .

He would do anything for his grandmother—he even allowed her to call him Willie—but he drew the line at kidnapping Americans. He walked quickly outside, through Essex Court to St. James. Pitty would be watching with her binoculars, he was certain. But as he'd anticipated, there was no trace of the American in the black coat. She could have gone in search of Marlborough House, he realized as he tried to reconstruct their brief conversation. A brisk walk took him to the entrance of Marlborough House, but no pretty tourist stood entranced at its door, and the mansion was obviously closed. William turned and surveyed the area, just in case she was wandering nearby taking pictures.

There was no help for it. William crooked his finger, and a gleaming black cab pulled to the curb. There was another place the tourist had mentioned, unfortunately for him. He could return to the house and tell Pitty he couldn't find the woman with the pin, but he'd promised to do his best. "The Tower of London, thank you."

"Right, guv."

He leaned back in the cab and sighed. Pitty had insisted he come to London this month. There had been decisions to make about Thorne House, decisions that only he could make. "As the Duke of Thornecrest," preceded her every order. He was thirty-six, had been the ninth Duke of Thornecrest since the tender age of ten, when his father had fallen from the balcony of Kittredge Manor. His mother, always frail, hadn't lived to see her son's eleventh birthday. And his grandmother, with the authority only a dowager duchess could command, had taken over raising him.

He'd inherited his father's hearty constitution, his mother's dark coloring and his grandmother's common sense. The title had come with six estates, Thorne House, a massive bank account, the family jewels and a responsibility to carry on family tradition.

Which meant marriage and a son to be the tenth Duke of Thornecrest. Except the ninth duke had no intention of marrying.

No one he knew was happy being married. No one in his family had ever been happy. Landrys were accustomed to marrying the wrong people and being miserable for the rest of their lives and, possibly, right through eternity. Generations of once-bickering Landrys lay buried in the family tomb at Leicestershire. How they had ever managed to produce children he never knew, but for the past five generations there had been one child born to each Duke of Thornecrest, a son named William, the son to carry on the title.

Traditionally the duke and duchess parted ways after the birth of the child, to separate houses and separate sex lives. There was nothing about this family tradition that appealed to the present duke, however. If he must do his duty and produce the next duke, he would wait for a long time. A *very* long time. He doubted there would ever be a shortage of women in England who were willing to be a duchess and live an independent life.

Not everyone required love, William reminded himself. But he would like to live a life without bitterness and rancor, bickering and unhappiness. Was that too much too ask?

"THAT LOOKS like the stone in your pin," the middle-aged woman next to Kate said. She pointed to the yellow diamond in the middle of a crown labeled The 1820 Diadem. "But yours is bigger."

"Yes, I guess so." Kate tried not to smile too broadly. She didn't want to hurt the woman's feelings. She leaned closer to the glass, noting that the yellow diamond really did resemble the center stone of Aunt Laurabelle's pin. She'd never seen jewels so beautiful or so large as the ones in the royal crowns.

The woman shot Kate's pin another admiring glance. "Did you get it at the tower gift shop?"

"No. It belonged to my aunt."

"She's not the queen of England, is she?" the woman teased.

"No. Too bad, though." Kate moved slowly down the aisle as the woman beside her chuckled. She didn't want to miss seeing a single treasure in one of the most famous collections of jewels in the world. She'd read about it in the guidebook: "Dazzling and brilliant, the most precious stones in the world are one of London's most popular attractions."

She could see why, and she was glad she was wearing Aunt Belle's pin. In the Tower of London Jewel House, the gaudy brooch fitted right in.

This was fun. She liked having only herself to worry about, even though her family thought she was crazy to come here alone after she'd lost her job and her fiancé in the same month. She could enjoy ten days without anyone giving her advice, or trying to give her advice. She was free. While she toured London, she could forget about Jeff and the wedding that wasn't going to take place.

"It's a sign," Anne had announced when Kate had told her about the breakup. "And I never thought he was right for you." It was a sign, all right. A sign that she should take the trip she'd been saving for. Kate had taken her severance pay and put it into traveler's checks. She had the *Guide to London* in her black tote bag. Things could be worse. She could be in Rhode Island, standing in line to collect unemployment and reading the classified ads. Instead, she was one of many fascinated tourists filing through the collection of crown jewels.

She lingered at the display, soaking up the atmosphere and trying to absorb the history involved. When she stepped outside, the sky had darkened and a chilly breeze blew from the nearby Thames. The famous ravens were nowhere to be seen, but the White Tower loomed in the distance. Kate glanced at her watch. She'd spent longer in the Jewel House than she'd realized. She could make a quick tour of the famous landmark, then hit the gift shop before the tower closed for the evening. A hot cup of tea, a sandwich and an early bedtime would round off the day.

"Excuse me," a male voice said behind her.

Kate turned and saw the man who had talked to her in front of Thorne House. Tall and handsome, with piercing dark eyes and ruffled brown hair, he was easy to recognize. His skin was tanned, too, she noticed, as if he worked outside each day. Although his leather jacket looked about fifty years old and the jeans were worn, he didn't look like a thief or a rapist.

"You were able to see the jewels?" His gaze dropped to her pin, then returned to her face.

"Yes. They're wonderful, aren't they?" She took a step toward the White Tower, wondering why he was speaking to her. After all, her skills as a temptress were practically nonexistent. He fell in step beside her.

"Yes," he agreed, then hesitated as they walked together. "Do you mind if I join you? I, uh, particularly enjoy the collection of medieval armor displayed there."

Kate didn't know if she minded or not. She was pleased to be talking to this good-looking man with a British accent, but she didn't want to be accosted in

London, especially not in her first hours in the city. "Oh, well, I don't think . . ."

"I'm sorry. I'm being quite rude." He stopped, blocking her path. "I'm William, er, Will Landry. Duke of Thornecrest."

Her pretty mouth dropped open. "Did you say Duke of Thornecrest?"

He bowed slightly. "At your service. I apologize for frightening you. I certainly didn't have any intention of doing so. It's just that . . ." He hesitated.

Kate knew she was gullible, but could he expect her to believe that she was talking to a duke? She wondered how far he'd go with his story. "Just that what?"

He gazed down at her with serious dark eyes. "My grandmother felt terrible that someone who wanted to see Thorne House so badly should be denied the opportunity."

"Your grandmother," she repeated.

"You don't believe me." He didn't look too pleased that she wouldn't take his word for it.

"Not exactly. Doesn't it seem a little odd to you?"

His stunned expression almost made her laugh. Then he pulled his wallet out of his pocket and showed her identification. "Satisfied?" His voice was haughty.

"Yes." Someone should have warned her that dukes were dangerously handsome, with charm oozing out of every aristocratic pore. Maybe if she'd been prepared, she wouldn't be acting like an idiot. Maybe she'd be able to think of something intelligent to say. "You *live* in Thorne House?"

William stuck his hands in his pockets. "I live north of here, actually. In the country. I'm here in London on business. Would you like a tour? I'd, er, hate to have you miss seeing the house. Even in its present state."

"You followed me all the way here to tell me your grandmother wanted to show me the house?" Dukes were kind, too, she added to her mental list of lordly characteristics.

"You did say you were coming to the tower. Are you enjoying yourself?"

"Very much."

"Well? Would you like a tour?"

"Yes, thank you." She would have to call Anne, no matter how expensive it was. She had to tell someone she'd met a duke the first day she was in London.

He looked at his watch. "We don't want to miss tea."

Tea. Very British, and on her list of things to experience. Still Kate hesitated. She'd never been the kind of woman who was pursued by handsome men. Not like Anne, who, with her long legs and golden blond hair, could attract the attention of every male within sight. Or Carol, a voluptuous redhead with a degree in philosophy and three charming children. Or Terri, sleek and trendy, who owned her own beauty salon and had twins with genius IQs. Being short and ordinary looking didn't attract the kind of men who looked like William Landry.

He might be a duke, all right, but that didn't mean she was getting in a car with him. "I'll meet you there. I'd like to get a picture of the White Tower."

The duke gave her a thoughtful look. "I'll walk with you instead," he replied. "That is, if you don't mind the company. I haven't seen the armor display since I was nine."

They walked in silence for a few minutes, until Kate stopped to take a picture of the tower. "Would you mind?" she said.

He frowned. "Mind what?"

"Taking a picture of me by this sign?"

"Oh, I suppose not." He didn't look enthused, but he held out his hand for the camera. Kate stood quietly for a moment until the duke finished taking the picture and handed the camera back to her.

"Thanks. What do I call you? Sir? Your Grace? Lord?"

He winced. "'William' is fine."

Kate turned and held out her hand. "I'm Katherine Stewart. From—"

"Rhode Island," he supplied. "I remember." He took her elbow and guided her toward the whitewashed stone building.

Much later, after examining every display of armor from each period in the history of Great Britain, Kate conceded it was time to leave. "You don't want to have to hurry your visit to Thorne House," William advised. "And my grandmother will be expecting us."

"That was incredible. All that armor was so old. And the jewels—" Kate's delight overcame her shyness. "I can't believe what I've seen in just one day. I could go home tomorrow and be happy."

"Tomorrow?" His voice sharpened. "You're leaving tomorrow?"

"No." She dared another look at him. Yes, he really was handsome. She wasn't hallucinating from lack of sleep. "I just arrived this morning. Everything they tell you about jet lag is true," she confided. "It's not easy

staying awake, but I don't want to waste any time
sleeping when I could be seeing things."

"How long are you staying?"

"Ten days. I booked the British Airways London
Showcase special."

"What on earth is the Showcase special?"

"You get airfare and six nights in a hotel, but I added
three extra nights. It includes a full English breakfast
every day and one free dinner. Plus tickets to two
shows, a seven-day card for the subway and a free afternoon bus tour of London."

"That sounds like quite an ambitious week for you."

"It's a dream come true to be here, so I don't want to
waste a minute."

Americans, he thought, were all alike. Awestruck by
England's history and royalty, they stayed in perpetual
motion. He hurried her past the tower gift shop and into
a cab. He'd played tourist long enough.

In a few minutes Pitty would see the brooch, realize
it wasn't what she thought it was and send the American on her way. With her guidebook, her maps, her
schedule and the oddest bit of jewelry he'd ever seen.

2

THORNE HOUSE SAT near the end of Essex Street. As the taxi came to a halt in the elegant street, Kate pulled her camera from her bag to record the moment. She stepped out the of cab and framed the doorway, with its graceful columns on either side of the polished mahogany door.

The duke climbed out of the taxi that had come to a stop behind her, so she turned and took a picture of him, too. She wanted to make certain she had pictures of everything so when she returned to Rhode Island a complete record of her London vacation would exist in four-by-six-inch color glossies.

The frowning duke paid for both taxis, despite Kate's objections, and waved her toward the door, which he unlocked and opened.

"I apologize for the state in which you find my home," he said, following her into the wide hall. The marble floors were partially covered by a plastic runner, and the paintings on the walls were draped with fabric to protect them from the dust. The duke led her from room to room, and Kate was amazed at the opulence of the interior of the London mansion. Even with much of the furniture draped with white sheeting, Kate could see that the rooms were beautiful. He took her into one of the completed areas, the museum, with its displays of Meissen and Berlin porcelain, a gold-plated silver dinner service and various swords used by Thornecrest dukes in a confusing number of wars; then on to the drawing room, its tall windows overlooking Green Park and the gallery, which ran the length of the house and held an impressive display of priceless paintings.

Kate listened to the duke's entertaining comments about the history of the family. He was an accomplished tour guide, yet he didn't sound bored reciting what must be familiar stories about his ancestors.

"Are you ready for tea?" He finally stopped in front of a discreet elevator door.

"Yes," she gulped, and followed him into the elevator, which took them to the private apartments on the third floor. The large living room, done in green and ivory, was only slightly less opulent than the downstairs rooms.

A large elderly woman rose from the emerald-striped sofa. Her gray hair was piled on top of her head in a bun, and her bright pink suit was classic and, Kate guessed, very expensive. Large pearls gleamed at her ears and throat and draped over a massive bosom. She held out her hand and Kate hurried to take it. She wondered if she was supposed to curtsey and resisted the impulse.

"Katherine, I'd like you to meet my grandmother, Patricia Landry, Duchess of Thornecrest and family tyrant. Pitty, this is Katherine Stewart, from Rhode Island."

"Thank you for inviting me to your home," Kate said, wondering why the elderly woman gave her such an assessing look. "I've enjoyed seeing it so much."

"It is my pleasure, of course," the dowager replied. She gestured to Kate to sit in an ivory wing chair as she settled herself back on the sofa. "I'm sure my grandson told you—"

"I've asked Kate for tea," William interjected. "I told her you were distressed that someone who wanted to see it so badly be denied a tour of Thorne House." He turned to Kate and smiled. "May I take your coat?"

Feeling out of place, Kate stood once again and removed her coat with William's assistance. She wished she'd worn her knit dress. The black stretch pants and matching fuzzy sweater certainly weren't dressy enough for tea, but at least her suede boots were acceptable. It helped, she told herself, that knits didn't wrinkle, so no one would know she'd been in the same clothes since yesterday.

"What an interesting pin," the duchess declared as William handed the coat to the tiny maid who had appeared like magic. "It's very unusual. Where on earth did you find it? In London?"

"You're the second person today who has asked me that. It was a gift from my great-aunt."

The dowager turned her gaze back to Kate. "Then it's a family heirloom?"

"Yes."

"It's much too valuable to be worn on the streets of London," the old woman declared. "You should deposit the brooch in a vault."

"Oh, don't worry. It's not valuable." Kate smiled, hoping the intimidating dowager's expression would soften.

"Except to you," William pointed out.

"Yes," she said, watching the satisfied smile he gave his grandmother.

The dowager sniffed, then looked past Kate's shoulder. "Mary, we'll have our tea now. Miss, er, Stewart will be joining us."

William poured something into a glass on the mahogany sideboard, then settled himself in a low chair and crossed his feet on the matching striped hassock. "We toured the tower, Pitty. It was just as I remembered."

"Was it?" She ignored him and turned back to Kate. "Tell me about yourself, my dear. Where do you come from?"

"Rhode Island."

"And what brings you to London?"

"I'm on vacation."

"By yourself?"

"Yes." The dowager looked at her as if waiting for her to explain.

"I just lost my job," Kate added reluctantly, "so I took the severance pay and my savings and came to London."

"How interesting," Pitty declared, seeming to mean it. "And why did you come to Thorne House?"

Kate felt a little silly explaining she might be distantly related to these regal-looking people. "There's a family story that says my grandmother's family came from here."

Pitty raised her eyebrows. "Do go on, dear."

"An Englishwoman, supposedly related to one of the dukes of Thornecrest, married a cattle rancher. Have you ever heard of a relative like that?"

"No, I don't think I have. Perhaps you're mistaken."

"Maybe. You know how family stories get exaggerated." Kate hoped she wasn't mistaken at all. She rather liked the romance of it all.

Pitty wasn't through with her questions. "Tell me, my dear, what are you going to do while you're here?"

Kate smiled. "As many things as possible, I hope. I've planned all sorts of tours."

The maid entered the room and placed the tea tray on the low table in front of the elderly woman. Besides an ornate silver service, there were three delicate cups and saucers, and several plates piled high with tiny sandwiches and little cakes. Pitty poured and William jumped up to help serve a cup of tea to Kate.

Tea with a duchess. Imagine. Odd that people still had tea in the afternoon, just like in books. Kate felt herself begin to relax as she sipped the hot tea. That tiny bed at the St. Giles was going to feel wonderful. She wondered how many hours she'd been awake without sleep. Twenty? Twenty-three?

"Katherine?"

She looked up, realizing she hadn't heard what had been said. She smiled at William. "Sorry. I just realized how tired I am. What did you say?"

"I told Pitty that you enjoyed the Tower of London."

Kate looked back to the duchess. "Yes. Very much."

The old woman selected a dainty sandwich and put it on her plate. "And the Jewel House? What did you think of that?"

"I've never seen anything like it."

"No?"

The duke hurried to join the conversation. "I remember that Father took me to see the display of armor. I don't think it's changed in the least."

"William must show you the rest of London, Katherine. There are so many things you must see."

"I believe," the duke drawled, "Miss Stewart has her trip completely organized."

"That's true," Kate said. She set the teacup on the lace-covered table to her left and then pulled the sheaf of papers from her bag. "Tomorrow is Buckingham Palace, Hyde Park and the rest of the Covent Garden area. And I especially want to see Carlton Terrace."

The duchess held out one hand. "May I?"

Kate handed her the papers. The old woman perused them, then handed them to William, who also read them.

Kate waited for him to look up. "What do you think? Have I missed anything?"

He handed them back to her, a stunned expression on his face. "I think," he said slowly, "you must be a very energetic young woman."

"I don't want to leave anything out." She tucked her itinerary safely inside her tote and reached for her teacup. She felt a little wobbly; maybe it was time to leave before she did something to embarrass herself. Still, this was her one and only chance to have tea in an English mansion, so she really shouldn't hurry off, and the luxurious room was oddly comfortable.

"I don't think you should worry about that," Pitty replied, giving Kate another assessing look. "Would you like a watercress sandwich?"

"Thank you." Kate took the fragile china plate offered her. "You've been so nice. When I came here this afternoon, I didn't expect anything like this."

William raised his eyebrows and turned to glance at his grandmother before smiling blandly at Kate. "Neither did I."

"IT'S THE PERFECT solution." Pitty stood at the windows that faced Essex Court and watched their American guest step into the black taxi. The jewel twinkled briefly before Katherine disappeared inside the cab. "I'm sure it's the same piece of jewelry the third duchess wore to the coronation. The painting is in the Long Gallery at the Hall."

"I doubt that it's the same brooch." William stepped away from the window, poured himself another brandy and took a swallow. Pitty must be growing senile after all. It was a shame, too. The old girl used to be sharp as a tack, and now she was obviously slipping.

His grandmother sank back onto the couch, looking quite determined. "But the diamond..."

William turned to glare at her. "You don't know whether or not that stone is the diamond, or if that brooch is the original Thorne piece. It could be a very good copy. It takes a jeweler to distinguish between real and fake now."

"Which is precisely my point," Pitty agreed. "We have to find out, and what better way than to take Katherine into Longmire's and have them look at the pin? Discreetly, of course. I will prepare them ahead of time."

"And how do I explain a trip to an exclusive jewelry store, Pitty?"

"She'll believe anything you say, of course." Pitty sniffed. "You're a duke and she's ... an American."

An American with a tempting smile and a body that would stop London traffic. When she'd removed her coat, he'd almost dropped it on the carpet. "I've followed her, brought her home, given her a tour of the house and served her tea, for heaven's sake. And now you want me to play tour guide?"

"Yes. Just until we find out if the stone is real or not."

The stone couldn't be real. Nothing so priceless could exist for over one hundred and fifty years without being discovered. "I'd planned on leaving tomorrow, you remember. The refurbishment is almost finished, and I've made every decision there is to make about furnishings and wallpaper. Gaylord has selected several pieces you'll find interesting and can aid you with any other problems that come along."

Pitty didn't flinch. "I want the brooch. I want the Thorne Diamond returned to the family once and for all."

He could feel his plans to escape London slipping away. "And if this American brooch is not the real one? What then?"

"If it's not the Thorne brooch, I'll promise to stay out of your affairs for the rest of my life. Which isn't for long," she reminded him. "I'm—" She stopped, making William chuckle.

"You almost slipped. Someday I'm going to find out how old you really are."

Pitty gave him an arch look. "On the death certificate, I presume."

He ignored the comment, knowing she wanted him to feel guilty enough to agree to her plan. "I'm going to change. I've already missed lunch with Jessica. I should ring—"

"I already did that," Pitty informed him, pouring herself another cup of tea. "I told her you would be in touch with her later and apologized for the inconvenience. She was most understanding."

"I'm sure she was." Pitty wanted him to marry, and she would not want him to alienate a very eligible candidate for the position.

"Jessica's a lovely girl. She'd make a wonderful duchess." Pitty sighed. "Naturally you have to own the brooch first. It guarantees your marital and lifetime happiness, and that, of course, is what I wish for more than anything else."

William didn't want to talk about the damn brooch for one more minute. "I'm going to change."

"The Smithfields are joining us for dinner at eight," she reminded him. "You remember them, don't you?"

"Yes. I suppose they are bringing their niece with them."

"She's a sweet girl."

"I am not interested in 'sweet girls,'" he snapped before leaving the room. It was almost archaic, William decided as he headed down the hall to his rooms in the east wing. His grandmother would have been at home in another century, where men spent their days buying horses and gambling, and women's only purpose was to produce male children. But this was the twentieth century. There was no butler, no calling cards and no valet to care for the closet full of expensive clothes he only wore in London. He entered his enormous bedroom and considered his situation.

Jessica could wait, and so could Thorne Hall. He didn't want to remain in London, but here he was. And there were Pitty's feelings to consider. If owning that ugly brooch would make her feel better, then he would have to do his best to acquire it. After he found out its authenticity and value, it shouldn't be difficult to convince the green-eyed American to sell.

Katherine Stewart should wear emeralds anyway, he thought, stripping off his clothes. Or tourmalines, to match those eyes. And nothing else, he decided, remembering the fit of her sweater and the way her pants clung to slim legs. Perhaps spending a couple of hours with her wouldn't be such a hardship after all. He'd go along with Pitty's scheme, up to a point. Just to humor the old girl.

After all, what were the chances that the Thorne Diamond would turn up on his doorstep after two hundred years? All he had to do was prove the stone was glass and he could return to the hall, blessedly alone and confident he'd done his best to make an old woman happy.

And, just to be cautious, he'd call Pitty's physician in the morning.

THE BOXY BLACK TAXI stopped in front of the St. Giles, and the driver waited patiently as Kate sorted through her British money. The array of coins was confusing. Embarrassed, she held out a palmful of coins and let the driver take what he needed.

"And the tip," she reminded him.

"Thanks, luv," he said, nodding his head.

Kate stumbled out of the cab and headed toward the door of the hotel. She managed to collect her luggage, check in at the desk and stumble to the elevator that took her to her sixth-floor room. She didn't bother to unpack. Her mind, foggy from lack of sleep, swam with images of London. In twenty-four hours she'd flown from Boston to England, walked through the streets of St. James and Piccadilly, toured the Tower of London and met a duke and a duchess. Thorne House was as she'd imagined, splendid and elegant.

Tea with a duchess. A walk with a duke. Would anyone believe it? Kate rummaged through her suitcase and found her flannel nightgown and her cosmetics bag. She brushed her teeth in the tiny bathroom, then undressed quickly and snuggled under the covers of the single bed. The room was small, so small that it would be difficult to get out of bed if the chair wasn't pushed in place under the desk. A television hung from the ceiling, and a small window stood in the corner by a simple armoire.

Kate pulled the covers up to her chin and took a deep breath. The queasy feeling that had plagued her since Jeff broke their engagement had eased a little, and her heart didn't ache as much as it had before. She'd been right—the change of scenery had been good for her already. Despite everything that had happened in the past two months, she'd survived. Kate smiled as she closed her eyes; she was no glamour girl, no sexy twenty-one-year-old with long legs and masses of hair. Jeff had made his choice; now it was up to her to get over it. She'd lost her boyfriend and she'd lost her job, but she'd plan the rest of her life the same way she'd planned this trip to London: she'd cram as much as she could into every day and not worry about what anyone else thought.

KATE HESITATED at the entrance to the large breakfast room and handed her room card to the maître d'. After the complimentary buffet breakfast, she planned to wander down Charing Cross Road, see Carlton House Terrace and walk around Covent Garden. She'd read there was an antique market there on Mondays. Then there was the free bus tour this afternoon, something else included in the package from British Airways she didn't want to miss.

The man nodded and handed it back to her. "The Duke of Thornecrest is waiting for you, miss."

She hadn't expected to be told the duke was in the St. Giles dining room. "The Duke of Thornecrest?"

The maître d' pointed to a table for two against the far wall where William Landry sat reading a newspaper. Kate walked carefully around a table full of rolls and cold cereal to join the duke. He stood when she approached, an apologetic smile on his handsome face.

"I hope you'll forgive me," he said, waiting for her to be seated before he joined her. "I was told this was the best way to catch up with you this morning."

"But how did you know when I'd be here?" *And why are you waiting for me?*

The waiter approached, asked her if she wanted coffee and poured a foaming liquid into her cup. It looked hot and strong, but why was it foaming? She eyed it with suspicion and took a cautious sip. Not bad, she decided, just a little different.

"Your schedule." He folded his paper and set it aside. He wore dark slacks and a charcoal sweater over a gray-striped shirt. No jeans and scruffy jacket today, she noted. Today he looked as if he was indeed an English aristocrat. "You showed it to me yesterday afternoon."

Kate placed her napkin in her lap and took another fortifying sip of coffee. "Okay, you read about my travel plans. Why—"

"Why am I here?" he finished for her, his smile charming. "I expected you to ask."

"Consider yourself asked, then."

He leaned back in his chair. "Pitty insisted you required a tour guide. She says, um, she says you, er, have the look of a Landry, so you must be a member of the family through some connection."

"Then Aunt Laurabelle was right."

He frowned. "Aunt Laurabelle?"

"She gave me the brooch. She never had any children, and I was the niece closest to her."

"Aunt, er, Laurabelle is the person who told you the story about the relative who may or may not have come from London and may or may not be related to the Landry family?"

"Yes."

"I see." He eyed her with a thoughtful expression. "Pitty could be correct after all."

"It's nice of her to worry about me, but I don't think I'll have any trouble finding my way around London. I bought several maps and—"

"You're refusing me, then?" He looked disappointed.

"I'm sure a duke has better things to do than act like a tourist." This was one of the strangest conversations she'd ever had. How could she tell a duke she didn't want to spend the day with him?

"Actually I don't," the duke was saying. "I've been dragged to town for the refurbishment. Pitty pretends she needs my advice, when actually she just wants company. She thinks I spend too much time in the country."

"Do you?"

He smiled, showing a perfect set of white teeth. "Yes, thank goodness. Why don't we have breakfast and discuss the day ahead?" He looked at his watch. "It's only eight o'clock. There's plenty of time for you to decide whether or not you'll let me tag along."

"All right." She hated to eat alone. Besides, she and William were related . . . maybe. And she didn't want to be rude to someone who had gone out of his way to be nice to a total stranger. "I didn't mean to be rude."

William looked surprised. "You're not the one to apologize, Katherine. I'm forcing my company upon you because my grandmother thinks you need a guide." He gave her another charming smile, one that warmed a little corner of her frozen heart. "Now you're forced to converse with a stranger over breakfast, which must also tax your patience."

"I don't . . ."

He slowly stood up. "I'll tell Pitty I couldn't find you," he offered, tossing his napkin on the table. She noted his rough hands, the callus on his right thumb. A duke who preferred farming, he'd said. A man who would rather be working outdoors than sight-seeing in London. Kate knew she couldn't send him away even if she wanted to, which she didn't. The idea of touring alone had seemed better in Rhode Island than the reality of being in London with no one to talk to. "Please, sit down."

He paused, one eyebrow raised, waiting for an explanation.

"I hate to eat alone."

"So do I." He gestured toward the buffet. "Shall we?"

"Sure." Kate crossed the crowded room and eyed the selection of food. Aside from the stack of yogurt cups, everything in the heated bins looked as if it contained at least one hundred grams of fat. She didn't have to diet anymore, she reminded herself as she took a plate from the stack at the end of the table. She didn't have to squeeze her size-9 body into a size-7 wedding dress in order to look good in the photographs.

She could let herself go, at least for a week. Kate speared a thick sausage and dropped it on her plate. She was on vacation, so she might as well enjoy herself.

"Ever had bangers before?" William said from behind her.

"Bangers?" She glanced up at him. Was the duke turning kinky now that she'd invited him to stay for breakfast?

His eyes twinkled. "Sausages." He nodded toward her plate. "Take two. I think you'll like them."

She did as he suggested and watched as he helped himself to four of the sausages. She skipped the eggs, selected a bagel, a small helping of fried potatoes and a bowl of canned apricots. Tomorrow she would be sensible and eat yogurt, but today she'd laugh in the face of cholesterol and eat "bangers" for breakfast. After all, she was in England, alone. She could do anything she wanted.

HE WAS INSANE, Will told himself. He'd let Pitty talk him into this, and now he had talked Katherine out of dismissing him. He could have left, he *should* have left when he'd had the opportunity. Pitty would have had no choice but to accept the fact that the Thorne Dia-

mond hadn't returned to London after all. And pigs
would fly, he thought, spearing his final portion of
sausage.

"We'll walk down Charing Cross Road and then
through Covent Garden before heading to Buckingham Palace," Kate said as she reached inside her
purse. "I've looked at the map, and it doesn't look too
far away."

"It's not." But Longmire's and Pitty's expectant jeweler were in the opposite direction. "What about a tour
of St. James Square?"

"I did that yesterday, on my way to Thorne House."
She studied her list, her chestnut hair brushing the paper.

"Oh." He should be able to think of some way to
convince her to walk through that area again.

"It was very nice," she assured him.

"If you like jewelry, there's a store there you
might—"

"I don't think I'd be able to afford anything in there."
Katherine turned her green-eyed gaze on him, and all
thoughts of Longmire's flew out of his head. He'd always preferred pale blondes with long legs and a certain level of sophistication. How could he explain his
fascination with a luscious little redhead—or was it
more brunette?—who wolfed down four bangers for
breakfast and admitted she didn't have eight generations of her family's money to spend on baubles. "I read
that Covent Garden has an antique market today."

"Antiques," he repeated. "You like antiques?"

She shrugged. "I like old costume jewelry and little
things like that. You never know what you'll find, you
know."

"Oh, I know." William stood and picked up his coat. "I'm quite aware of that, you see."

Katherine smiled at him as she stood up and hooked her purse straps over her shoulder. "Then maybe you'll find something at the market, too."

"Perhaps," he conceded, still wondering why the sudden attraction to green eyes. Of course, the luscious little body didn't hurt, either.

He waited downstairs in the lobby while she went to her room for her coat and the indispensable guidebook. When she returned, the brooch was pinned to her coat lapel, as it had been yesterday. William didn't know whether to be relieved the pin was still available or annoyed at the sparkling reminder of his grandmother's failing mental capacities.

"Is something wrong?"

William realized he was frowning at her. He made an effort to tear his gaze from the pin and force his lips into a smile. Or at least what he hoped looked like a pleasant expression. "No. I was thinking about our morning. You don't mind walking? It's a bit cloudy, but I doubt we'll get wet."

"I'd rather walk," she agreed, so he led her out to the sidewalk and turned toward Oxford Street and Charing Cross Road. Somehow he'd have to figure out how to stroll by Longmire's. He could invent an errand, he supposed. With a few turns they could be in St. James instead of Covent Garden, and she'd never suspect him of deliberately confusing the directions.

He hadn't counted on the damn map. Katherine pulled it out and examined it at regular intervals, despite his assurances that he knew the way to the Covent Garden Market.

As they headed down Garrick Street, Katherine was clearly enjoying herself, he realized. She studied the buildings and the assortment of people around them with undisguised interest as they negotiated the narrow sidewalks. They passed the theater where *Miss Saigon* played, then spotted the open square of the marketplace. Off to the left was a covered area crammed full of tables and people.

"That must be it," Katherine said, and increased her pace toward the flea market.

"Stay with me," William warned, conscious of pickpockets. Under the roof were crowded paths between tables laden with silver, jewelry and the oddest assortment of things he'd ever seen. It looked as if everyone there had dumped the contents of their cellars and attics on their tables.

Katherine was thrilled. "Look," she said, pointing to a pile of silver spoons. "Do you think they're old?"

"Yes." And ugly. He hurried after her to the next table, where she glanced at an assortment of cracked teapots and ceramic figures.

"You don't have to stay in here," she said. "I could meet you outside in an hour or so."

"I'll stay." He wandered the aisles beside her, watching as she peered into glass cases of jewelry and eyed little boxes of Roman coins. At a corner table he picked up a silver candlestick with a distinctive pattern on its base.

Katherine turned. "What did you find?"

"I'm not sure." The markings were right, but would it match the one at the Hall?

"Thirty pounds will take it home," the ruddy-faced owner said, nodding toward William.

"I'll think about it," he replied, setting the candlestick back on the table. Katherine peered into a glass case filled with rings, and William saw the man's eyes widen as he spotted the brooch.

"How much is that one?" Katherine asked. The man blinked and turned his attention to the display case.

"Which one, dearie?"

"The tiny one with the pearls and . . . emeralds?"

"Victorian," he announced, putting it into her palm. "Late Victorian, and those are emeralds. Very delicate," he added. "It suits you."

"How much?" She slipped it on her middle finger and admired the effect.

"For you, forty pounds."

"Twenty," William interjected.

"Thirty." The owner grinned. "Final offer, guv."

"I'll think about it," Katherine said, handing the man the ring.

"Come back soon if you want it," he cautioned as he replaced it in the case. "Rings like this don't last long, especially at that price."

"Thank you anyway," she said, and crossed the aisle to the next row of tables.

The red-faced man turned to William. "So, you must be Thornecrest."

"How—"

He shook his head and continued in an awed voice. "I didn't think the Thorne Diamond existed. Just read about it, y'know. Lost in 1814, wasn't it?" He looked over at Katherine, in conversation with a lady selling lace. "But not lost after all. Plain as day, staring at me. Couldn't believe my eyes, I couldn't."

He had to mean the brooch. "It's a copy," William explained.

"No." The man shook his head again. "That's the real thing, it is." He handed William one of his cards. "Give this to your lady, in case she changes her mind about the ring. I'm here every Monday."

William took the card, but he didn't want to discuss the odd brooch any longer. "It's not what you think."

The man winked. "She must be the future duchess. No wedding ring yet, I see, but it's only a matter of time, according to the legend." He winked once again, and William turned away. He hurried to catch up with Katherine, who had moved on to another display of costume jewelry. So Pitty wasn't the only one who recognized the brooch. He eyed it curiously as Katherine chatted with a lady who had necklaces for sale. The central yellow stone winked and sparkled, even in the dim building. White diamonds and emeralds surrounded the large stone, with rays of yellow topaz shooting to the corner in an ornate metal setting that looked to be painted.

"What do you think?" Katherine asked.

He glanced up. She held up an amber necklace, a simple strand of beads that matched the highlights of her hair. "Lovely," he murmured, picturing the beads on naked skin.

"Ten pounds?" She looked uncertain.

"A bargain," he assured her.

"It *would* be a perfect souvenir from Covent Garden."

"What about the emerald ring?"

"I can't have both, and this is cheaper."

"Then you should buy it," he insisted. "It suits you."

She handed the woman the money and then fastened the necklace around her neck as William watched. The heavy beads fell above her breasts and gleamed against the black sweater.

William gulped. He'd broken a major rule today. Shopping with a woman was something he'd avoided up until now, although Covent Garden wasn't exactly Regent Street and Kate didn't appear to expect him to pay for the amber beads. Still, he wasn't acting like himself at all. Since yesterday, since that damn pin had appeared, his life had been turned upside down.

It was time to take control.

3

"WE'LL HAVE a light lunch at Green's Oyster Bar, near St. James Street," William announced as he turned from the gates of Buckingham Palace. "They serve a delicious selection of seafood, especially oysters. I'm sure you'll enjoy it. Then we could do some shopping in the area."

Kate's heart sank. She hated to refuse him, but she had all the oysters she wanted in Rhode Island and she was certain she couldn't afford to buy anything in the exclusive neighborhood of Thorne House. "Oh, I'm sorry. I booked an afternoon tour and I have to be at Russell Square by two-thirty."

He frowned at his watch, then at her. "What sort of tour?"

"A bus tour of London. It came with the package, so I'd hate to miss it." Kate didn't believe that he was disappointed she couldn't have lunch with him. She knew the duchess had coerced him into spending the day with her, which only embarrassed her a little. Her ego had been so badly trampled that a little bit of pity from a duchess couldn't make much difference. Kate rummaged through her bag and found a map. "There's a tube stop at Russell Square, so getting there should be easy."

"Where are you supposed to meet this tour?"

She glanced through her papers hurriedly. His frown made her nervous. "At the Royal National. I think it's right around the corner from the tube."

He took her elbow. "I'll go with you."

"On the bus? I think they're booked ahead—"

"Not on the bus," he said. "To the hotel."

"You don't have to do that, William." She liked calling him by his first name once in a while. It made her feel that he was almost . . . friendly. Which, she concluded, glancing at his stern expression, was probably just an illusion. Although he could be charming when he wanted to. It was easy enough to like him when he was trying to be likable. He had the kind of lean strength that made her long to curl up against him.

She reminded herself he was a duke.

"Yes," he replied, taking her elbow and turning her around. "I know."

William seemed familiar with London's subway system and got them to Russell Square easily. When they emerged from the stairway, Kate stopped on the sidewalk and tried to get her bearings.

"This way." He pointed to a street on their right. "We can get a bite to eat at the hotel."

"Just a minute," she said, and started off toward a grassy park where people were lounging on benches and eating out of cardboard containers. "There must be a place over here."

They rounded the corner and saw a line in front of a low building. The smell of fish and french fries wafted through the air. "Fish and chips!" She grinned happily. "Let's get some."

He stopped. "Here?"

"Sure. Why not?"

William looked as if he could have given her a few hundred reasons, but she turned away before he could say anything. He followed her along the paved path to the building. Tables and chairs dotted the concrete patio in front of the restaurant. "You get a table," Kate told him. "I'll get lunch."

William opened his mouth to protest.

"No, really." Kate stopped him. "It's my treat. You've been so nice, it's the least I can do." The line was moving quickly, and she was soon able to order two plates of fish and chips and two soft drinks. The young man behind the cash register took her money and handed her two large cups of soda, then told her she'd have to wait a bit for the food. The line for lunch had lengthened, and the cooks looked harried.

Kate crossed the patio to where William sat. She set the drinks in front of him. "The fish will be here in a minute. I think they're pretty busy."

"We could still go to the hotel. They're sure to have a restaurant—"

"And eat inside? No way." She went back to the building to wait for their lunch. When she returned with two cardboard plates piled high with fish and french fries, William eyed it hungrily.

"Here," she said, dropping plastic forks and paper napkins on the table. "Help yourself."

"Thank you." He arranged his napkin in his lap and picked up the fork. "I appreciate the lunch."

"You're welcome. I know this morning wasn't your idea of a good time."

"Why would you say that?"

"I'm sure dukes have better things to do than play tour guide to distant American cousins." She speared a piece of fish and sampled it. "Mmm, good," she murmured. "This is something I've always wanted to do."

"Dine in Russell Square?"

"Eat fish and chips in England."

"Does this live up to your expectations?"

"Yes." An outdoor English lunch with a handsome duke? She couldn't hide her smile. What a story she'd have to tell when she got home.

"I see you're wearing your pin again today. It matches the color of the daffodils."

Kate reached to touch it. "Yes. I think it brings me luck."

"Why?"

"I'm not sure. Back home things kept going wrong, and since I've been in England *nice* things have happened. If I were a superstitious person, I'd think Aunt Belle's pin had something to do with it."

To her surprise, he didn't smile, just regarded the pin with a serious expression. "Some people might believe so."

She turned her attention to her lunch. "What brings you luck?"

He shrugged. "I have no idea."

"Maybe because you're a duke you don't need any."

"I've never thought about it," he admitted, pushing his empty plate away a few inches. "I suppose most people would consider me fortunate."

"What about your parents?"

"Both dead. Pitty—my grandmother—raised me."

"I'm sorry."

"It's not as tragic as it sounds."

She didn't believe him. "Do you have any brothers or sisters?"

"No. I come from a long line of only children." A bitter smile accompanied the casual words, and Kate's heart twisted in sympathy. "And you? I suppose you come from an enormous family."

"Three sisters, all married, all living in Rhode Island. My parents died four years ago." He waited for her to continue. "Everyone thought I was crazy to come to England instead of job hunting."

"Did you need to 'get away' from something in particular?"

"My fiancé called off our wedding last month, which was bad enough, but I worked as a computer programmer for his father, so I lost my job, too."

His perfect eyebrows rose over his brown eyes. "A bit of bad luck," he agreed. "You enjoyed computers?"

"No, not really." She took one more bite of french fry and wiped her lips with her napkin. "I was looking forward to being married and having children and making pot roast and apple pies." She made a face. "I know you're not supposed to admit to something so old-fashioned, but I really was excited about having babies and pushing strollers and all that."

"I'm sure you'll find someone else," he assured her.

"What about you?"

"Me?"

"Don't dukes get married?"

"Not this one."

"Maybe I've read too many romances, but don't dukes have to get married and have a son to carry on the family name and all that? Like Prince Charles and his two sons. Don't they call them the 'heir and the spare'?"

"I've heard that," he drawled. "But I have no desire to marry. The dukes of Thornecrest have had marriages more turbulent than Prince Charles's and Princess Diana's. I have no desire to carry on that particular family tradition." He looked at his watch and stood. "You're going to miss your tour unless we leave now."

Together they gathered up the garbage, deposited it in a nearby trash can and walked along the path to the street corner. It was an odd place to say goodbye, but Kate held out her hand and he shook it briefly.

"Thanks for everything," she said, meaning the words. "You didn't have to be so kind, and I appreciate your taking the time to show me around."

"It was nothing," he said, looking down at her.

"It was quite a bit," she countered. "I'll be sure to tell my family that I met a real-life duke and he was very nice."

He smiled, a very charming smile that made Kate's breath catch in her throat. "And I'll be sure to tell my grandmother you enjoyed yourself," he promised.

"Thank you." She forced herself to turn away and cross the street as the light conveniently turned green. The mild spring breeze blew her hair across her face as she adjusted her purse straps on her shoulder and headed for the hotel. She fought the urge to turn back and wave, knowing that the Duke of Thornecrest was certain to be heaving a sigh of relief now that he was finished fulfilling his grandmother's idea of family duty. She'd write the duchess a note next week and thank her for being so thoughtful.

"YOU LET HER GO? You let her walk away? What on earth were you thinking?"

The Duke of Thornecrest tossed his coat to the maid, then loosened his tie. He went to the sideboard and poured himself a drink. Scotch, he decided. He was definitely in the mood for Scotch. "Should I have tackled her in the middle of Bloomsbury and dragged her to Longmire's?"

Pitty sniffed her disapproval. "You should have kept her with you. What if something happens to the pin?"

He took a grateful swallow of whiskey. "On a bus tour?"

"I'll have one of those," she said, nodding toward the glass of whiskey. "With a little ice."

William fixed her a drink and crossed the living room to hand it to her. She wore a lime green sweater-and-skirt set today. The color made his head ache. "Here," he said. "You can drown your sorrows with this."

"I don't have any sorrow. Except one." She took a sip, then studied her grandson. "You smell like fish."

He ignored her. He wasn't going to tell her that he'd had a very pleasant lunch at a dingy metal table in Russell Square, or that he hadn't been able to take Katherine to a restaurant around the corner from the jeweler's. He wasn't going to tell her he was disappointed that Katherine's wonderful figure stayed hidden under her black coat, or that when she smiled at him and shook his hand he'd felt a jolt of lust that nearly knocked him to the sidewalk.

"You're going out tonight?"

"I'd planned to, yes." Actually he'd made no plans, thinking he would be home at the Hall tonight. And Pitty knew it, too.

Pitty's fingers drummed on the sofa. "And the diamond? Where will that be? Do you remember?"

Unfortunately he did. "I imagine Miss Stewart will be wearing her brooch to the theater tonight. *Miss Saigon*, I believe."

"Then you will escort our little cousin to the theater."

"It would be impossible to get another ticket to *Miss Saigon* this late in the day, Pitty."

Even as he said the words, he knew he was wrong. She had that familiar determined look on her face, the look he'd first seen when he was ten years old and a solicitor had told her she was too old to raise a child. She'd stared at the man, with her "queen face," as he'd called it, until the solicitor stammered an apology and hurried from the library. Pitty had remained his guardian until he'd no longer needed one.

"Nonsense." She reached for the phone and began to dial. "I'll take care of everything."

"She's going to think I'm a stalker," he grumbled. "A lunatic. A lust-crazed aristocrat out to shadow her every move."

"Quiet," Pitty ordered, then turned her attention to the voice on the other end of the phone.

William stood in front of one of the long east windows and finished his drink during Pitty's conversation with one of her cronies. He should never have come to London. He was accustomed to having his own way, of being in charge of his own life, until Pitty decided to interfere. She used his affection for her shamelessly, knowing full well he could deny her nothing. Now she'd involved him in a wild-goose chase over the ugliest brooch in Britain...with one of the most appealing women.

"You now have box seats for tonight's perform-ance," Pitty declared, replacing the receiver. "Miss Stewart will be enchanted."

"She's not my type."

"Of course she isn't." Pitty chuckled. "What an out-rageous thought! This has nothing to do with match-making, my dear. We're restoring a family heirloom to its rightful owner."

"You?"

Pitty shook her head. "You. There have been no happy marriages since the gem disappeared genera-tions ago. It was a wedding gift from the mother of the first duchess, you know. And rumored to have been part of Edward the Confessor's coronation crown."

"*If* it is real, Pitty."

Her expression was wistful as she looked up at him. "I pray it is, Willie. Then you can settle down and have sons. I've made a list of eligible women for you, so take your time—"

"Do not continue, Pitty. A dozen brooches wouldn't make me marry Jessica or anyone else, for that matter. Landrys have a poor history for that sort of thing, as well you know."

Pitty shrugged and finished her drink with one long swallow. "Once we own the brooch, the rest will take care of itself." She glared at him. "I thought you prom-ised to help me."

"Up to a point," he agreed. "And then I call your physician."

"There is nothing wrong with my mind, William. I'm as sharp as a tack, and you know it." He noticed her hand shook as she set her empty glass on the table.

"Perhaps," he teased, knowing she expected it. He didn't want to embarrass her by letting on he'd seen her trembling hand. "You'll need your wits to convince Katherine to allow me to accompany her to the theater tonight."

"Ten pounds says I can do it."

"Ten pounds it is," he agreed.

"And will you take her to dinner afterward?"

"Don't push your luck. I'll see her safely to her hotel, nothing more."

"That's enough," his grandmother declared. "I'm perfectly satisfied with that."

"Why don't I believe you?"

Pitty didn't answer. Instead, she stretched out on the couch and closed her eyes.

He went to his room and found the list of names propped against his pillow. Twelve women Pitty thought suitable for the position of Duchess of Thornecrest. Jessica's name was at the top; the Smith-fields' youngest granddaughter was next. The others were no more than acquaintances, although three bore the surnames of Pitty's oldest friends. William didn't know whether to laugh or curse. It was obvious he must prove the pin was a fake or fend off prospective brides for the rest of his life.

"HAVE YOU EVER SEEN *Miss Saigon?*"

"No. I've always wanted to." This was going too far, Kate decided. The duke and his grandmother didn't have to make sure she had good seats to the theater. He didn't have to escort her. He didn't have to look so handsome as he strolled beside her across the St. Giles's utilitarian lobby.

"You're upset," William declared, opening the door onto the street. "I told Pitty not to call you."

"You did?" So he hadn't wanted to take her to the theater after all. Which was no surprise, she realized, ignoring her disappointment.

"Yes." He took her elbow and guided her across bustling Oxford Street. At seven it was dark, but the city was alive with people. Kate shivered, noting the dampness that had come with the night. "I thought you would find the suggestion an invasion of privacy."

"She told me it would be a favor to her to keep you company."

"I assumed it would be something like that." When they were safely on the sidewalk on Charing Cross, he looked down at her, a worried expression in his eyes. "I thought we'd walk, but if you're cold we can hail a taxi."

"I'd like to walk. I get to see more of the city that way."

"You're not tired?"

"I took a nap after the bus tour," she confessed. "I think I'm still fighting the time difference."

She'd slept until Pitty had called, asking her help with her "stubborn grandson." She worried about him, the elderly woman had confided. Worried that he was lonely in London, that he would grow so bored he would return to the country ahead of schedule, leaving Pitty with no one. Kate didn't believe that story for a minute. William's grandmother had something else on her mind, or maybe she was simply eccentric. Whatever the reason, Kate had decided she'd be crazy to turn down an escort to the theater.

"What about you?" she asked. "What does a duke do in London in the afternoon?"

"A duke takes care of business," he replied.

"Farm business?"

"Yes."

"There must be quite a bit of it."

"Yes. And Pitty requires help with the redecoration of Thorne House."

"She must value your opinion."

"That's what she'd like me to believe. Tell me what you saw today," he suggested, easily changing the subject.

"I think we saw everything." She smiled in the darkness. "We spent a lot of time admiring the bridges."

"Were you suitably impressed?"

"Of course." She liked him when he relaxed. When he teased her she forgot he was a duke and enjoyed him as a man. A man, she realized, feeling the warmth of his hand on her arm, who was definitely attractive. One of the most handsome men she'd ever seen. He was also rich, polite and kind—perhaps they were requirements for an aristocrat. Well, maybe not kind. William Landry might be an exception. Or maybe she'd read too many historical novels.

They wound through the streets of the Covent Garden area until the Drury Lane Theatre was in sight. The ornate lobby was thick with people, but Will led her through the crowd and up a red-carpeted staircase and down a narrow corridor to a curtained box. The usher checked their tickets, sold William a program, wished them a good evening and left them to their seats. Kate thought she'd died and gone to heaven.

"May I take your coat?"

"Thank you." She forced her attention away from the crowds pouring into the theater. Another first for Kate Stewart: an evening of London theater. She unbuttoned her coat and stood. William helped her slide it from her arms and placed it carefully on a nearby chair.

"I notice you're not wearing your brooch—" He stopped in midsentence as he turned back to her, his gaze focused briefly on her chest. "It's quite lovely where it is now, of course," he murmured, lifting his gaze to her face.

She felt her cheeks grow warm, the curse of pale skin and hair with a touch of red to it. She'd worn her new chestnut knit dress, a simple design with a V neck, long sleeves and a hem just above her knees. She'd pinned the brooch to the point of the V, and that, along with gold earrings, was her only jewelry. Jeff had always said her eyes were her best feature, stating her breasts were a "little too obvious." He'd also said he wished she was taller, that she lighten her hair and wear more makeup.

To hell with him.

"Thank you." She lifted her chin, hoping William wouldn't realize he'd flustered her.

He gestured toward her seat, and she took it, anxious for the show to begin. She didn't want to feel attracted to him. It was too embarrassing, too much a cliché.

William removed his own coat, revealing a perfectly tailored charcoal suit and striped white shirt. The tie was a conservative paisley in shades of gray and maroon. "Two kings were shot in this theater. George II and George III. Are you familiar with English history?"

"A little. The guidebook said this is where William IV first saw Mrs. Jordan."

"So you're a romantic." He sat down and leaned back in his seat to look at her. "Love at first sight, happily ever after."

He made it sound like something horrible. "Of course. I'm the person who wants children and pot roasts, remember?"

"Yes." His gaze dropped to the brooch, then moved back to her eyes. "What would you do with a great deal of money, Katherine?"

"Travel," she replied easily. "Buy a house, maybe. Help my nieces with college, things like that."

"You've given it some thought."

"Rhode Island has a lottery. I play it sometimes."

"When you feel lucky." He nodded toward the brooch. "Maybe that will bring you luck, as you said."

Kate touched the middle stone with her index finger. "I think it already has."

"And if it was valuable?"

"If it was valuable, I'd have to make sure I took very good care of it."

He opened his mouth to reply, but the theater darkened. Kate settled back in her seat and prepared to enjoy her first taste of London theater. She couldn't believe this was only her second day in England. She didn't know how it could get any better than this.

William leaned toward her. "Is something the matter?"

She realized she'd sighed too loudly. "I was just thinking, I could go home tomorrow and be happy."

He gave her an odd look, then smiled. "I'm glad you're enjoying yourself so much."

"Thank you for tonight," she whispered as the curtains rose. "I'm sure your grandmother put you up to it, but it was nice of you to go along with it."

William turned startled brown eyes in her direction. "Nice?"

"Yes, you *are* nice," she stated, turning her attention to the stage. "Whether you like it or not," she added softly.

HE LIKED IT. Too much. He liked the way her hair glinted red in the sunlight and darkened in the dim light of the theater. He liked the way she smiled at him and the way her green eyes lit up when she teased. He liked that damn brown dress and the soft, enticing cleavage above the sparkling pin. He didn't care for her choice of restaurants or her ambitious tourist plans. He didn't think she'd forego a tour of Hampton Court for three days in a suite at the Ritz.

She might believe in romance, but he believed in lust.

Kate cried at the end of the show. He handed her a handkerchief and waited for the tears to subside. He'd seen this particular show with three other women, and all of them had wept a little, careful not to smear their eye makeup. Kate couldn't be worried about eye makeup, he decided, not with the flood of tears pouring down her cheeks.

He cleared his throat. "Are you all right?"

She took a deep, shuddering breath. "It's been a rough month."

"I can see that." He waited, pretending a patience he didn't feel. He hoped she would get herself under control soon, before people began to stare.

"It's just that I thought it was all planned." She sniffed. "My life, I mean. Oh, the wedding was all planned, too, but that was just going to be one day out of a whole lifetime of wonderful things."

"Like children and pot roast," he added, longing to put his arms around her. He drummed his fingers on his thighs. "Would you like some air?"

She nodded but she didn't move. "He said I didn't interest him anymore, that he was bored already."

Bored? William's gaze was incredulous. The man must have been an idiot. "Do you still love him?" For some reason it was important to know.

"No." Katherine winced. "I'm too angry."

"What's wrong with being angry?"

"It hurts."

"Oh." He waited as she wiped her tears and took another deep breath. "Would you like some dinner? Londoners dine after the theater," he explained, hoping to distract her. "Or we could have coffee and dessert somewhere, if you prefer."

"I'd like that."

He stood and helped her with her coat. He patted her shoulders in what he hoped was a reassuring gesture. She didn't appear to mind. They discovered a shop nearby, with tempting pastries displayed in the window. They drank coffee topped with whipped cream. She offered him a bite of her chocolate truffle cake; he shared his éclair and told scandalous stories of royal affairs, pleased with himself when the sparkle returned to her eyes. He hailed a cab, bundled her inside and saw her safely to the front door of the St. Giles.

"Wait here, please," he told the driver, then escorted Katherine inside, through the empty lobby and around the corner to the elevator. Kate hesitated before pushing the sixth-floor button.

"Thank you again," she told him, her lips curved into an appealing smile. "I enjoyed the day."

"So did I." He meant it, too. He put his hands on her shoulders and stepped closer, lowering his head. Surprise flickered across her face, but then his lips touched hers and he closed his eyes. What began as a simple good-night kiss turned into something more, something he didn't want to stop. He'd expected warmth and sweetness; he hadn't expected heat and passion. He felt her lean closer, and he moved so their bodies touched. Despite the layers of wool coats between them, he could sense the heat from her skin and feel her tremble when his tongue parted her lips.

He stopped, blinked, released her. He managed to say good-night; she said something equally polite in response, but he didn't bother to listen. He turned and walked out of the hotel before he could change his mind.

He arrived at Thorne House in minutes, not long enough to forget the feel of Katherine's body against his. Not long enough for the aching tension in his body to ease.

Not long enough to decide what he was going to do about her. William Landry didn't seduce American tourists, especially not vulnerable "cousins" recovering from broken hearts and canceled weddings.

He should run; he should hide. He should return to the manor and bury himself in spring-planting preparations. He should go skiing and have sex with Jessica or someone else equally sophisticated, someone who wouldn't expect anything more than discretion and the good sense to leave the bedroom before dawn. Katherine would expect sweet words and promises and happily-ever-after.

He didn't know why he was thinking this way about a woman he'd only met yesterday. A woman who wore a pin that drove his grandmother insane with curiosity and longing. He didn't care about the pin. The damn piece of jewelry was what had gotten him into this mess in the first place.

"Well?" Pitty peered out from behind her bedroom door. He could see a strip of crimson chiffon from her neck to her toes.

He stopped in the wide corridor, knowing he was trapped. He unbuttoned his coat and reached up to loosen his tie. "Don't put any more lists on my bed, Pitty."

"I just thought—"

He cut her off. He was not about to discuss her crazy marriage plots. "Did you have a pleasant evening?"

"Very nice, thank you." Her tone was hurt. "Did you?"

"Yes."

"Will she sell the brooch?"

"I don't know. And you're not buying it unless you know it's authentic."

"Tomorrow," Pitty declared. "Tomorrow you will drag her into Longmire's and have the pin appraised. I don't care how you do it. This foolishness can't continue."

He'd like to drag Katherine somewhere, but it wouldn't be to a jeweler. But he did agree that this couldn't continue. He had to get control of himself. "I believe she's taking a tour tomorrow."

Pitty looked at him with her queen face. "Have her postpone it," she ordered. "This has gone far enough. I will call her in the morning and explain everything."

"No," he replied, looking her right in the eye. "You won't. I will take care of this from now on, without your interference. I will determine whether or not the diamond is real, and if so, I will purchase it. From now on you are no longer involved."

"But—"

"Good night." He watched her eyes widen, then her mouth closed in a thin line and she shut the door. William didn't linger in the dark hallway. He wanted to get to his rooms and a cold shower. He heard Pitty's door open again and he stopped, bracing himself for another argument.

"Willie!"

He didn't turn around. "What is it now, Pitty?"

Her voice was triumphant. "You owe me ten pounds."

KATE EYED the telephone and tried to remember the time difference between London and Rhode Island. Five or six hours? Forward or backward? What a day it had been: buying an antique necklace in Covent Garden, eating fish and chips in a park and watching *Miss Saigon* with a handsome bachelor who just happened to be a duke. She'd never met anyone like William Landry before, and she wasn't sure how she would describe him. Self-contained, naturally. Cynical? Sometimes. Polite to a fault and dangerously charming, definitely.

Kate climbed into the narrow bed and turned off the bedside lamp. She pulled the covers over her shoulders and snuggled into the pillows. William Landry was also an experienced kisser and a very passionate man. He kissed her as if he found her irresistible, which made her smile into the darkness. His suit probably cost more than she made in a month, and yet he'd treated her like a princess. Correction, he'd treated her like a desirable woman. And that's what made him so very interesting. Apart from all the other things, that is.

It was over. She'd toured Thorne House as she'd intended. She'd had the unexpected bonus of William's company while sight-seeing and at the theater this evening. She'd thanked him; he'd kissed her. She'd said goodbye, not good-night. There was no reason to think she'd ever see him again.

All the same, it had been quite an adventure.

4

KATE WOKE EARLY, before the alarm buzzed at six o'clock. She wrote postcards, took a quick shower and put on her black stretch pants, suede boots, brown turtleneck and ivory cardigan. The amber beads added just the right touch, she decided, hooking them around her neck. After all, she was going to a castle and a palace today. She wanted to be comfortable, but she didn't want to look like a frump. She'd enjoyed dressing up last night, enjoyed the flattering expression on William's face when he saw her.

Jeff had looked at her like that in the beginning. Then he had stopped being charming, and his criticisms had begun. Maybe a lot of men were like that. She put on her makeup, fixed her hair and checked to make sure she had enough money. After a hearty breakfast of bangers and bagels, Kate hurried to the lobby. The tour bus stopped at the St. Giles at eight-fifteen, but the concierge had advised being early. A familiar figure stood by the fern in the corner, tall and lean in jeans and a patterned sweater, a raincoat folded over one arm. He smiled a little sheepishly as she walked over to him.

"What are you doing here?"

"Spending the day with you," William replied. "If you'll allow me."

"Did your grandmother put you up to this again?" She refused to be the object of the dowager's pity any longer.

He shook his head. "She was still in bed when I left. Supervising the refurbishment has worn her out, I suppose."

"I'm heading to Hampton Court and Windsor Castle. The tour bus should be here any minute."

"Could I possibly talk you into postponing that until tomorrow? I thought you might like to see Kensington Palace, where Princess Di lives. I'll even take you to some of the stores where she shops." He gave her a charming smile and waited for her answer.

"I can't. I'm sorry." She certainly was, she thought. "But I already paid for this tour, thirty-eight pounds, and it's only offered twice a week in the winter. This is my only chance. We also have lunch in a real pub, so I wouldn't want to miss it."

"And what about Kensington? You shouldn't miss it."

"It's on my schedule for Saturday." There. He could go home to his mansion and tell the dowager that he had done his best, but their American cousin already had plans for the day. She was a little tired of people feeling sorry for her.

"Too bad," he said, and looked as if he meant it. His disappointed expression shocked her. "I thought you'd enjoy tea at Browns. It's one of the best teas in London."

"Really?" Kate almost wavered, but caught herself in time. Even a duke couldn't change her plans at the last minute. And shouldn't. "I'll have to remember to go there before I head home."

"You would enjoy it." He looked at his watch. "Excuse me for a moment," he said, and moved through the crowd toward the concierge.

Kate felt sorry for him. He looked a little lonely. It mustn't be easy living with his grandmother and having his house torn up, and he obviously missed his farm.

He returned within minutes, a satisfied expression on his face. "There. I've booked a seat on the tour, too."

"You booked a seat on this tour? How?"

"With a credit card, Katherine. It took no great skill." He lowered his voice. "Should I apologize for kissing you last night?"

"No, of course not."

"Good." He smiled with satisfaction. "I didn't intend to. Actually I intend to do it more often."

A warm feeling snaked through her chest. It was foolish to believe him, but it was fun to pretend. "Are you flirting with me?"

"Definitely." His gaze flickered to her coat. "You'll be glad you brought that. It's a bit chilly out this morning."

"So we're discussing the weather now."

"To kill time," he explained. "To distract you until the bus arrives so you won't have the opportunity to send me away."

"Look," she began, trying to resist his teasing smile, "you don't have to look out for me. I'm twenty-five, old enough to tour England by myself. You and your grandmother don't have to worry about me, you don't have to spend your day on a bus, you don't have to—"

"But I have tickets for *Phantom of the Opera* to-night," he protested. "I thought you would enjoy it, since you like romantic shows."

"*Phantom?* In London?" She stared up at him. How was she supposed to resist that?

He looked surprised at the question. "Why, yes. At Her Majesty's theater, on Haymarket. Do you already have a ticket?"

"No. I tried but I couldn't get one."

William looked very pleased with himself. "Then—"

"Tour bus to Hampton Court and Windsor Castle!" a man announced from the doorway. "Anyone here for the Evan-Evans tour?"

Kate raised her hand. "We are."

"Come on, then," the gray-haired man said. "We've many stops to make before we're out of London."

William followed her onto the huge tour bus and sat beside her near the front. She folded her coat over her lap and turned to him. "Why are you doing this, William?"

"Call me Will."

"Tell me the truth." She waited, and the bus roared to life and lurched into first gear.

"The truth," he repeated. He looked over her shoulder toward the window for a long moment before turning back to her. "How about this? My grandmother is matchmaking again, and I am avoiding her *and* the women she's proposing as candidates for duchess. It sounds archaic, and it is. She's like that, though. Immersed in another century."

"And you don't want a duchess?"

"Not in a million years." He grimaced. "I am the last man in England anyone would want to marry."

She didn't believe that for a second. Gorgeous and charming William Landry would have trouble keeping women away from him even if he wasn't a wealthy aristocrat. She tried not to laugh. "I would think a lot of women would want to marry you."

"Oh, for the money. And the estates." His eyes twinkled. "I know you're teasing me, but really, I have no intention of marrying anyone. Pitty continues to try, and I continue to, ah, stick to my guns."

"Until you have to resort to hiding out on a tour bus." Kate couldn't help but laugh. "You expect me to believe this?"

"Yes, I do." He didn't seem to mind her laughter. In fact, he leaned closer. "If you will help me." She waited for him to continue. "Let me take you to Kensington tomorrow and to the theater tonight. The less time I spend in Thorne House the better. I would prefer to play tour guide for another day."

"I have a lot of things to see," she warned him.

"I know. I saw your list, remember?" William relaxed against the seat as the bus stopped to pick up more people. So far, the only men on the bus were the driver, William and the tour guide, who'd announced he was Richard and "anxious for everyone to have a jolly day."

"Think about it," William said. "You'd have your own private tour guide."

Tempting, but Kate didn't believe he was telling the whole truth. "And what do you get?"

"The company of a beautiful woman."

"Stop it," Kate said, embarrassed. "Don't make fun of me."

"Who's making fun?" He touched her chin with his index finger and lifted it slightly. "The man who broke your heart is a fool," he declared. "He didn't deserve your apple pies or your children."

Fortunately, the tour guide began to point out London landmarks, and Kate didn't have to reply. She pretended to look out the window as they passed Westminster Abbey, but her thoughts were centered on the man next to her. He had asked to spend the rest of the week with her. She was going home Tuesday, one week from today. For a few days she would see London with a duke, an Englishman who obviously knew his way around. Knew enough to get theater tickets to sold-out shows, at least.

Knew how to kiss.

He'd made her feel sexy and pretty and lighthearted. He'd made her forget about Jeff. She didn't even miss him anymore, which was a relief.

Kate turned away from the window to find William's gaze upon her.

"Still thinking?" he asked.

"Yes."

"That's not very flattering. I thought you'd feel sorry for me and agree immediately." There was a light in his dark eyes that showed he was still teasing her.

Again she wanted to laugh. "You're not an easy person to feel sorry for."

He sighed. "Would bribery work?"

"No!"

"I thought not." He pointed out the window. "That's the Victoria and Albert Museum. Have you been inside yet?"

Kate peered at the enormous stone building as the bus whizzed by. "Not yet. I suppose your family donated some of the artifacts?"

"A few."

She shook her head. "We lead different lives, William."

"'Will,'" he corrected. "My friends call me Will."

Kate looked at him and nodded. "Call me Kate, then."

"I didn't think you were a 'Katherine.' It's much too formal a name for you."

"I've always been Kate, or Katie," she admitted. "How long have you been a duke?"

"Since I was ten."

"*Ten?* Can a child be a duke?"

"Of course. When my father died I inherited the title."

"No wonder."

His raised eyebrows were a question.

"No wonder you're the way you are," she said. "Very duke-ish."

Will's shoulder touched hers. "Be quiet, Kate, and enjoy the scenery."

She quit teasing him and concentrated on looking out the window as they passed through the same suburbs she'd seen coming from Heathrow Airport. Soon the houses disappeared, replaced by rolling green hills dotted with trees. Richard pointed out different sights, including the island where historians agreed the Magna Carta was signed. When the bus rolled down the straight road to Windsor, Kate took her camera from her bag and took a picture. The bus pulled into the parking lot, and everyone on the tour followed Richard up the hill to Windsor Castle.

"Unbelievable." Kate framed the castle in her lens and took another picture.

"Come on," Will said, putting his arm around her. "Richard said to meet him at King Henry's Gate in two hours." He handed her a map. "Here's another souvenir for you."

"You've been here before, haven't you?"

"Yes. Not informally, though. I feel as if I'm on vacation."

"Stand over there," she ordered. "I'll take a picture of you with the tower in the background. Then you'll *really* feel like you're on vacation."

He did as he was told.

"Cute couple," an elderly lady told her companion. "I always like to see the young people enjoy themselves."

Will winked at Kate and took her hand. "Now we're a couple."

"If only she knew that I was just doing you a favor."

He chuckled, then tugged her along the path to the main building of the enormous, sprawling castle. It was too big, too impressive to seem real, and Kate hadn't expected to walk through what had been a walled fortress. They toured the State Apartments, but the paintings were gone from the walls. Stored since the fire, they would be rehung when the renovations were complete.

Will declined to join her in the gift shop, preferring to wait outside on the bench and watch the guards parade in the grassy quadrangle that separated the public area from the private wings.

"What on earth could you find to purchase in there?" he asked when she stepped out of the small stone building.

"Lavender bath gel, grown from the queen's garden, for my sisters." She pulled one of the boxes from the paper bag to show him. "It smells wonderful," she explained.

"Did you buy one for yourself?"

"Yes. And wait till you see this." She held up a small tin replica of the castle. "It's filled with candy."

"How . . . interesting."

"Come on." She tugged him from the bench. "Let's go to the chapel. Kings are buried there."

"Something to look forward to," Will muttered, but his smile was good-natured as he stood beside her. "You love this, don't you?"

"I'm having a *great* time. What about you?"

He draped his arm over her shoulder as they walked around the building. "I'm finding this highly educational."

Kate didn't believe him, but it wasn't her business if the man wanted to spend his day acting like a tourist. She'd heard the English could be eccentric, and William Landry proved it.

HE LOST HER in the Clock Courtyard, named for the large timepiece towering above the grassy square. He knew where she was, or at least, he knew where she'd eventually end up. Nothing in the Hampton Court gift shops would escape her notice. So he wandered around the brick walkways of the enormous palace built by the powerful Cardinal Wolsey and eventually given to Henry VIII. He remembered visiting Hampton Court long ago, with his father. It had been a bright summer day, unlike today with its overcast sky and bitter March wind. There had been a ceremony of some kind; his father was an honored guest and hadn't seemed to mind the crowds or the long speeches.

Now family duty brought him once again to Hampton Court. If Kate Stewart owned the Thorne Diamond, then it was his duty to protect it. It was his responsibility to see that it was returned to the family where it belonged. Tomorrow he would discover once and for all if the brooch was real, *if* he could continue to convince Kate that he needed her company. The odd thing about all of this was that he actually enjoyed showing her around London.

His friends would think he'd lost his mind. He could be skiing. He could be in the Bahamas, where the Westons stayed every March. He'd joined them last year for a week for a house party that revolved around tanning one's body and drinking as much rum as one could hold.

Somehow it paled against purchasing lavender bath gel and tin castles. Besides, it was the least he could do for Pitty. She'd have spent too much money purchasing a questionable heirloom if he hadn't stepped in to prevent her.

Now Kate would be shopping again, and he would wait outside the building for her to find him. She hadn't stopped smiling all day, except once, when she'd studied the portion of boiled cabbage on her plate at the pub. He'd teased her into sampling a bite, but she hadn't liked the taste.

"Will?" Kate came up behind him. "I lost you. Sorry. There was a gift shop off the Tudor Kitchens, and I couldn't resist—"

"More bath gel?"

"A poster," she informed him. "And I bought myself a coffee cup." She attempted to balance the bag under her arm until he reached out to hold it for her. She unwrapped a white cup with gold lettering and the palace seal. "Pretty, isn't it?"

"Very." He peered into the bag. "What else?"

"Books, postcards and cute little pencil erasers for my nieces." She wrapped the cup in its tissue paper and placed it carefully in the paper bag. He insisted on carrying the bag, then took her hand and led her toward the gate.

"Have you seen everything you wanted to? We have to be back at the bus in about fifteen minutes."

"I've seen a lot," she told him. "I'll bet you could spend days here and not see everything."

"Yes, I'm sure that's true. If it was warmer, we could walk to the maze."

"I'll have to come back here someday."

It was natural to hold her hand and stroll through the courtyards like vacationing lovers. He really didn't know what had come over him. Tomorrow, he promised himself. Tomorrow, no matter what, he would find out the truth about the stone. After that he would make his excuses, say goodbye and return home. Nothing Pitty could say would stop him.

THE YOUNG WORKMAN with the mustache and the large shoulders finally found the box she wanted, the one marked Personal, 1800s. He carried it into the elevator and rode with Pitty to the third floor, then set it on the floor of her sitting room. The family correspondence had been packed away for safekeeping several years ago, and the box was covered with a thick layer of dust. Pitty eyed the dirty carton with distaste, then braved the dust to slit the cord with her embroidery scissors. Something the American girl had said about a Landry woman going to America kept nagging her.

There had been boys in each generation, not girls. It seemed Thornecrest dukes were incapable of siring daughters, thank the Lord, since they were not at all prolific. Her husband had spent his enthusiasm and energy on polo instead of in the bedroom. Their own son had had too many women to bother his wife once he'd gotten her pregnant. Marion had given birth to Willie and kicked her husband across the county to Kittredge Manor.

Pitty peered inside the box at the stacks of ledgers. Willie needed someone to love him. After all, she wasn't going to live forever, and then what would he do? He'd need someone in his life, someone to warm his bed and his heart. Someone who would give him a son. If the legend was true, then he needed the brooch to guarantee wedded bliss.

Nothing else would do. And the foolish boy refused to believe her. Well, she'd just have to prove it to him. It was time to take matters into her own hands.

Pitty reached into the box and set the ledgers on the floor. Estate journals wouldn't tell her what she needed to know, but the old duke's journals might. If she could prove there was a daughter who left Britain, she might be able to convince William of the brooch's authenticity. He didn't seem to be making progress on the appraisal. She couldn't imagine why such a simple task had become so difficult. Well, William had always been a stubborn child.

She took one of the wide black books from the box and opened it to the first page. The date in the corner, January 1, 1809, was scrawled in a firm, masculine hand. She wiped her dusty fingers on a dainty handkerchief and began to read.

WILL FOUND HER there hours later. Her faded purple sweatsuit meant she hadn't left the house or received visitors, both of which were unusual. He entered the room and stepped around the piles of books near the door. "Pitty? Mary said you've been in here all afternoon. What are you up to?"

She looked up at him and cocked her head. "Where on earth have you been? You're rather windblown and ruddy."

"Never mind me." He cleared a spot near her, sat down and stretched his long legs in front of him. "I asked you first."

"I'm pursuing family history, obviously." Pitty pushed a pile of old ledgers toward him. "Your great-great-great-great-grandfather, the third duke, kept journals, of course."

"Why the sudden interest in—" he opened one of the ledgers and read the date "—1810?"

Pitty tried to struggle to her feet. "I'll tell Mary we'd like our tea now."

Will put his hand on her arm and tugged her gently back down. "I already did. You look as if you could use some refreshment."

"Very true, dear." She yawned. "I've been reading for hours. Your ancestor was rather wordy."

Will didn't try to hide his smile. "And what are you attempting to learn through all this . . . research?"

She shot him a despairing look. "About the brooch, of course. Our supposed American cousin mentioned a Landry woman who emigrated to America, but I could find no record of a daughter in the family bible, so I've been searching through some of the old papers."

Intrigued, Will flipped through the pages. "And what have you discovered?"

"I'm not sure." Mary's polite knock distracted her. "Just set the tray down here, dear. It's easier for me to stay on the floor, I suppose."

Will waited while his grandmother fixed her tea and consumed three sandwiches. He never knew what she was going to do next, but he doubted she'd learned anything that would link Kate to the family jewels. He fixed himself a cup of tea and wondered what Kate was doing now. Writing postcards? Admiring today's crop of royal souvenirs?

Pitty patted the book beside her. "The journal mentions a young woman who seems to be under the duke's care. I can't seem to discover who she is, exactly."

"Some poor relation, perhaps?"

Pitty shook her head. "I don't think so. He speaks of her fondly, though she appears to be quite a handful."

"Where does the missing brooch fit in?" He leaned his head back against the couch and closed his eyes. He'd probably walked fifteen miles today, which was not unusual for a typical day in Leicestershire. Maybe the gift shops were what had worn him out.

"She could have stolen it and run away to America. Or sold it to a woman who passed herself off as a Landry."

He yawned. "There were two sons. Did they both marry?"

"Yes." Pitty sighed. "Both unhappily, of course. The brooch had disappeared by then."

Will debated whether or not to tell her about the antique dealer in Covent Garden, and then decided she would only worry that the pin had been recognized. "Have you read all of these?"

"Only two. Help me up, Willie. I'm dining with the Beauchamps tonight and need to rest for a while. They have a lovely granddaughter, you know."

Will stood and obediently hauled his grandmother to her feet. "I think she was on the list."

"She'll be at dinner tonight. I told Phyllis that you might join us."

He kept his hand on her arm until she steadied herself. "I already made plans."

Her eyebrows rose. "With Jessica Wilton?"

They slowly made their way to the door. "No."

"One of the Weston girls? I prefer the tall one. She has . . ."

Will gave her his haughtiest look. "I'm not going to discuss this any further."

"Don't play the duke with me, young man," she warned as he guided her down the hall to her bedroom. "Neither your father nor your grandfather dared try, and I won't put up with it from you."

He helped her onto her bed and tucked an ancient wool throw around her until she was satisfied her feet would be warm. He went to the door and turned back to see her eyes closed already. Probably dreaming of old journals and young brides, he decided. This business about the pin had gone on for too long. Pitty would soon work herself into a state of nervous exhaustion, and she was too old for this kind of excitement.

It wasn't doing him much good, either. He was a little old for cold showers. Tonight he would see that Kate enjoyed Webber's show. Tomorrow he would have the pin appraised. He would explain everything to Kate and hoped she understood how important it was to prove to his grandmother the brooch wasn't really the Thorne Diamond.

He was tempted to purchase it anyway, since it brought Pitty such happiness. There would be nothing wrong in letting an old woman believe she'd found the answer to her prayers. When that was settled, he would wish Kate well and wave goodbye. She could tell her sisters she'd met a duke; he would smile whenever he thought of her.

He knew that would be often.

SHE WOULD HAVE PAID five pounds for a bath. Kate eyed the shower stall and knew it wouldn't soothe her aching feet. She wanted to soak in a hot tub for an hour or two and warm the chill that had settled deep in her bones. No wonder the English consumed such large quantities of tea. A cup of Earl Grey had to be the next best thing to central heating.

Kate settled for a shower, letting the water run as hot as she could stand. She didn't have a lot of time, just enough to put her souvenirs away in the armoire and dress for the show. She'd have to wear the brown dress again; she didn't have anything else suitable. Will would return in an hour and a half. She'd offered to meet him at the theater, but the suggestion had seemed to offend him.

He was so proper. So very reserved and self-contained, except when he'd kissed her last night, and even then she sensed his surprise at making the gesture. She'd been a little shocked herself. She hadn't expected an Englishman to be quite so . . . passionate.

She decided to wear the amber beads tonight and left the brooch pinned to her coat. William seemed to admire it; she'd caught him staring at it more than once. He'd probably just never seen anything like it before.

Kate chuckled at the thought of his grandmother's matchmaking. The handsome duke wouldn't be able to avoid marriage for long. He'd be walking down the aisle with some suitably aristocratic bride before he was much older. The elderly woman had had a very determined look in her eye, Kate remembered.

She wouldn't want to be in the way of something the dowager wanted.

5

"MORE WINE?"

"Please." Kate watched William wave the waiter to their table, and in minutes her glass was refilled. This evening was too good to be true. She eyed William over the rim of her glass. "You're not going to turn into a pumpkin soon, are you?"

"Excuse me?"

She sipped carefully, knowing it was the most-expensive wine she'd ever tasted in her entire life, in the most expensive restaurant and with a man who wore a Rolex on his wrist. "You know, like Cinderella. Turn into something else at midnight?"

"You're enjoying the wine, aren't you?"

She set the glass on the linen-covered table. A candle, surrounded by crystal and fresh flowers, lit the center of the small round table. "Very much."

"I'm glad."

Kate looked at him thoughtfully. "You've been very kind. I still don't understand why. And I don't believe it's all your grandmother's doing."

"She's a large part of it," he replied, meeting her gaze squarely. "But I've enjoyed our two days together, I confess, even though I didn't actually expect to do so."

"Honesty at last," Kate murmured, reaching once again for her wine.

"You don't think I've been honest with you?"

"No." She couldn't help teasing him a little. "You're not much of a tourist, no matter how hard you pretend. I thought the gift shops would do you in."

He shook his head. "I didn't mind, although I can't imagine why you find them so fascinating. Actually visiting Hampton Court again was quite a treat. My father took me there when I was six or seven, so it brought back pleasant memories."

"What was he like?"

William stared at his glass and didn't answer immediately. "A bit stern but kind. It's difficult to remember after so many years. He fell off a balcony in Kittredge Manor, his home at the time. He didn't believe in spending money on restoration, and the railing was rotten."

Kate swallowed, trying not to picture the outcome. "I'm sorry," she whispered. "That must have been terrible for you and your mother."

"They were separated at the time—another Landry tradition. She didn't live a year after that. I like to think she loved him, despite their differences."

"She married him. She must have felt something, at least in the beginning."

He shrugged. "Perhaps. My grandparents were no different. Pitty and her husband lived apart for thirty years, until he died of heart failure. She has always blamed—"

Kate waited, but he didn't continue. "Blamed what?"

"Nothing," he said. The waiter delivered their soup and made certain everything was to the duke's liking before leaving them to the first course.

"This is lovely," Kate said, picking up her spoon. "When you talked about dinner after the show, I never expected anything like this."

"I come here often when I'm in town. The food at Lorenzo's is always excellent. How is your soup?"

"Delicious." She looked past his shoulder to a crowd of people. A tall woman was staring at William. She spoke to the waiter and, when the man nodded, she tried to catch William's attention. "There's a woman waving to you," Kate said. "By the door."

William turned to see, then tried not to groan out loud. Jessica was smiling and making her way through the tables toward him. He had no choice but to toss his napkin on the table and stand.

"Darling," she cried, kissing him on both cheeks. "Where have you been? Have you been avoiding me on purpose? Leaving messages with Pitty is becoming a bit tiresome." Before he could answer, Jessica turned her wide smile on Kate and held out her hand. "How do you do," she crooned as Kate shook the offered hand.

"Kate, I'd like you to meet a friend of mine, Jessica Wilton. Jessica, this is Katherine Stewart, a, er, cousin from the States."

"It's nice to meet you," Kate replied, amused at the suspicious expression that crossed the blonde's face.

"My pleasure," Jessica murmured, then turned back to William and tossed her long hair over her shoulders before leaning closer to him. "We really must get together sometime soon. When you're not so committed to family obligations."

"I'll look forward to it," he said. Kate didn't think he sounded too enthusiastic, which was interesting.

Jessica waggled her fingers toward Kate. Diamonds sparkled on her right wrist. "Ta-ta!"

"Goodbye," Kate replied. She'd never said *ta-ta* in her life, and she wasn't going to start now. William sat down and resumed eating his soup.

Kate watched the tall woman join a group of young people at a corner table. The men were in expensive suits, similar to Will's. The women wore simple, sleek dresses and had simple, sleek hairstyles. One of the couples separated from the crowd and started toward their table. The woman was tall and athletic, the man short and stocky, with sandy hair and a beard.

"Kate? Are you looking at something in particular?"

Kate turned her attention back to Will. "I think you're going to get more company."

"This is a popular place after the theater." He shouldn't have brought her here. He'd wanted to impress her, not embarrass her. Damn Jessica.

He felt a strong hand clap him on the shoulder, and a familiar voice said, "Will! I thought you would have returned to the country by now."

Will stood, surprised and pleased. "Sam! I thought you were skiing. Hi, Paula." He shook Sam's hand and kissed Sam's wife on the cheek, then turned to Kate.

"And who is this beautiful woman?" Sam turned to Kate and grinned.

"Let me introduce you to some old friends, Kate." Sam didn't have to look so interested, Will thought. He made the introductions, noticing Paula's curiosity and Sam's unspoken approval, and once again explained that Kate was a distant American cousin. "Sit down," he offered, gesturing toward the empty chairs.

Paula hesitated. "We don't want to interrupt—"

"Just for a minute," Sam interjected, guiding her toward a chair. "The others won't miss us."

Paula shot Kate an apologetic smile and shrugged. "Do you come to London often?"

"This is my first time," Kate explained. "And I've really enjoyed myself."

"How wonderful! You must have Will bring you to Leicestershire. It's beautiful country, and we live nearby."

Sam agreed, his eyes twinkling. "Yes, Will. You must do that. We'll be staying close to home for the next seven months," he announced proudly.

"Congratulations," Will said, shaking his friend's large hand once again. He turned to Paula. "Congratulations. That's wonderful news."

"You're going to have a baby?" Kate asked.

"Yes. We're celebrating tonight, then heading home tomorrow."

"Now we'll leave you to yourselves." Sam stood, took Paula's hand and winked at Will. "Sorry to have interrupted your supper," he said, but he didn't look the least bit apologetic.

"I hope you enjoy your visit, Kate," Paula said. "Come to the country," she called as Sam led her away.

"Nice couple," Kate said. "Good friends of yours?"

"And neighbors, too." He couldn't believe Sam was going to be a father. He'd known the burly Scot since their days at Eton. It was difficult to picture him wearing one of those baby backpacks. Will shuddered.

The waiter cleared their dishes and informed them their entrées would be ready shortly. William leaned forward, unwilling to allow the evening to be spoiled by so many interruptions. "Did you enjoy the show? Wasn't the music beautiful?"

He was pleased when her green eyes lit up. "The music, the costumes, the voices, everything. It was more beautiful than I could have imagined."

"I never tire of it, either," he admitted. "It's one of my favorites."

"When I tell my family I saw *Phantom* in London, from box seats, they won't believe me."

"You have the program to prove it."

"Yes. Thank you for that, too."

He didn't want her thanks. He simply wanted her to continue to enjoy herself. He'd never met anyone with such enthusiasm for new places. Most of his friends enjoyed traveling, but they also expected luxury, entertainment and friends to amuse them. Kate's only expectation was to see everything she possibly could see.

Kate's attention had wandered back to the corner table. "Is your grandmother hoping Jessica Wilton will be the next duchess?"

"I believe her name is on the list."

She stared at him. "The list?"

"Yes. My grandmother left a list on my pillow. It contained the names of twelve women of which she approved." He couldn't help chuckling, forgetting that it hadn't been at all amusing at the time he'd discovered it.

"It's a good thing you have a sense of humor."

"I told her never to do it again."

"Yes, you did," a quavering female voice replied near him. The familiar voice grew louder. "In no uncertain terms, too, for all the good it did you."

He didn't want to look. He'd been so intent on Kate he hadn't noticed his own grandmother. It was hard to notice anything when Kate wore that dress with the low neck.

"Good evening," Kate said. "How nice to see you again."

She sounded as if she meant it, William realized. He came to his feet and greeted his grandmother. "Your nap revived you, I see."

Pitty frowned. She didn't like to be reminded of her need to take naps, and William knew it. She turned to Kate and inclined her head in a regal nod. "Katherine. How nice."

Will remembered his manners. "Would you care to join us?"

"No, dear. My friends have reserved a table. We saw *Grease* tonight."

"What did you think?"

"It was quite loud and quite energetic," Pitty declared. "Very American, of course."

"Of course," William echoed, trying to keep a straight face.

Pitty waved him back to his seat. "Do sit down, for heaven's sake. I wanted to ask Katherine something about her family history. How lucky I am that she is here tonight!"

She must have heard him make the reservations, William figured. This was no coincidence.

"I'd be glad to," Kate said.

"Do you happen to know the name of the woman— the Landry—who emigrated to America? Or the date, perhaps?"

"I might be able to find out. I'd be happy to send you any information I can."

"Thank you, dear. I would appreciate that."

"It's the least I can do."

"And where is your lovely brooch tonight?"

"On her lovely coat," William replied. "And here comes our lovely dinner."

"So nice to have seen you again," Pitty murmured to Kate.

William sat down and waited for their plates to be set in front of them. "I didn't know it would be like this," he apologized. "I thought we would have a peaceful supper."

"You didn't have to hurry her away."

"Yes, I did," he muttered. Next time he would select a more private, less popular restaurant. Next time?

"She must be lonely when you leave London."

"Not really. We spend part of February together in London each year, and she comes to Thorne Hall when she wants a taste of the country. She has a lot of friends around England. Her social life is quite extraordinary."

"But you are her only grandchild?"

"Yes."

"Then you should be nicer to her," Kate declared, picking up her fork.

He couldn't get any nicer, William fumed. He'd delayed his return to the Hall, he'd ridden a tour bus and eaten greasy fish and chips, he'd bought two theater programs, he'd kept his eye on the brooch throughout most of London's tourist attractions. He was the nicest grandson in Great Britain.

And he should be appreciated.

Kate distracted him with stories of growing up on a farm with acres of apple orchards. She made him laugh, made him want to take her in his arms. She made him want to hold her hand and whisper nonsense until the rest of the world disappeared. Instead, he ate dessert and paid the check and helped her climb inside a taxi when the evening was over.

He wasn't sure why, but it seemed natural to put his arm around her. When she turned to him to say something, he stopped her words with a kiss. It appeared to surprise her, but it seemed inevitable to William. Her lips were soft and warm. He held her closer; she twined her arms around his neck. He ran his tongue along her lower lip; she parted her lips to allow him entry. She tasted of chocolate, sweet and mysterious.

"All day," he breathed, lifting his mouth a fraction from hers, "all day I've wanted to do this." The interior of the cab was dark and intimate, and William's free hand swept through Kate's hair and along her cheek.

"We shouldn't—"

"I know." His lips found hers again, and the long kiss continued. Once again they parted and drew ragged breaths.

"Thank goodness the St. Giles is on the other side of town," he said.

Kate laughed, so he kissed her briefly once more. "Do you know where we are?"

"No. But I know I've never made a fool of myself in a taxi before." He grimaced. He didn't know what had gotten into him. He was usually more of a gentleman, more restrained.

"Well, neither have I." She attempted to straighten her dress. "Another international experience no one will believe."

"Why not?"

"I'm not exactly the type who makes men crazy with lust."

"You're not?" She could have fooled *him*.

Kate smiled. She thought he was joking, he realized.

"It's the dress, then," he declared, keeping his voice light. Her coat was open to reveal the amber beads draped over that tempting cleavage. Kate shifted and the yellow stone on her lapel blinked and winked at him. He closed his eyes briefly, trying to remember what he was supposed to be doing. The brooch. The legend. His grandmother.

He sighed, muttered an apology and released Kate. The taxi slowed, crossed Oxford Street and turned the corner to the hotel. "I'll come by for you at nine," he said. He helped her out of the cab and watched her cross the sidewalk and step into the brightly lit lobby.

"Essex Court, please," he told the driver. That cold shower was going to be a relief.

PITTY WATCHED Will hurry through the rain and into a taxi. She frowned. It was ridiculous to depend on taxis. She didn't know why he wouldn't spend the money on a car and driver. A perfectly nice Jaguar sat in a garage, too. Perhaps it was time for her to learn to drive, she mused. Wouldn't *that* drive poor Willie to the asylum? She dropped her binoculars and rang for Mary.

"Find that nice young man with the mustache," she said. "I need his help again."

Mary muttered something under her breath, but Pitty paid no attention. Katherine had looked quite at home at San Lorenzo's last night, and William had not been pleased when she'd interrupted them. Poor Jessica had looked daggers at both Will and the American. Yes, it had been quite a show.

This marriage scheme was not progressing the way she'd planned. William should have owned the brooch by now. Then he could have met the nice English women on the list she'd prepared, and been guaranteed marital bliss.

Unlike the rest of the Landrys, she mused. Her own William had been as worthless a husband as ever stepped over the Thorne Hall threshold, but he'd known how to turn one pound into five and had tripled the family fortune before he died.

Pitty lowered herself onto the couch and waited for the young workman. There were boxes to remove and boxes to fetch. She planned to find the answer to this family mystery soon, before William could make a fool of himself over the little American.

She didn't want her grandson to marry a mysterious American. Besides, Katherine was much too short to be a duchess.

KATE ROAMED around the crowded palace gift shop. The Duke of Wellington teapot was tempting, but it might be hard to get back to Rhode Island in one piece. This would be her last day with the handsome duke, Kate resolved. It was bad enough to have been a fool in Rhode Island, but to go international with her stupidity was even worse. Of course, she found him attractive. Who wouldn't? And charming. Who could be immune to his charm?

She could, Kate told herself. She had to. She was much too attracted to him.

Of course, that could be a rebound kind of thing. After all, her ex-fiancé was getting married in three days. She'd be expected to do something strange and reactionary. Like kiss a duke in a taxi.

Thank God her sisters knew nothing about this. She'd never hear the end of it. She selected three packets of floral bath salts for them. She could tell them this was what Di used, and they might believe her.

No more dukes, she promised herself. He'd been pleasant and polite when he'd escorted her through the dark rooms of Kensington Palace. She thought he might be a little embarrassed about last night, too. And regretting it, of course. The display of coronation robes had been interesting, but the real attraction would have been Di's wedding dress, no longer in the display. Being refurbished, no doubt.

She bought a postcard of the wedding dress anyway. Thank goodness she had been able to return hers before it had been altered. She'd lost her deposit, of course, but that was better than getting stuck with sixty yards of satin and lace that she didn't need. She'd tried to repay her sisters for their black off-the-shoulder gowns, but they wouldn't hear of it. They'd selected them, after all, with an eye to wear them again on special occasions.

She paid for her purchases and met William in the foyer. The rain continued to pour, so he opened a black umbrella and held it over her head as they stepped outside onto the paved walkway.

"Typical English weather," he said above her head. "You'll get used to it."

"I don't mind," she fibbed, feeling the cold seep through her damp boots. They weren't waterproof, but she'd worn two pairs of socks. "Where are we going next?"

"We're going to find a taxi. We'll head up Sloane Street and King's Road so you can see where Princess Diana shops. Then on to Harrods, if you would like to see the world's most famous department store. Wasn't that also on your itinerary?" He looked at his watch. "If you're not too hungry, we can skip lunch and have tea a bit later."

"You know, you don't have to do this," she said, looking up at him. A curl of damp hair hung over his forehead. He was just as attractive in the rain, she thought. "I'm perfectly capable of finding my own way."

"I wouldn't hear of it. Come on." He took her elbow and, avoiding puddles of water, hurried her to the side of the busy street.

Well, she'd tried, Kate mused. She scrambled into the boxy black taxi as if she'd done it all her life. Will climbed in after her, and they exchanged sheepish glances. It was a little too easy to remember what had happened the last time they were in a taxi.

"We're going to Antiquarius, 135 King's Road," Will told the driver, then settled back in his seat.

To break the silence, Kate asked, "Is your grandmother still matchmaking?"

"Yes. She offered to arrange a lunch date with someone today, as a matter of fact."

"And you refused."

He smiled. "I claimed a previous engagement."

"So you're really glad to be out in the rain?"

"Absolutely. I had an errand to do anyway. I have to stop at an antique market for a few minutes. Something I have to check on. Would you mind?"

"Of course not. It sounds like something I'd enjoy. Is it like the Covent Garden Market?"

"No," he replied. "But you might find it amusing."

Kate found it overwhelming. The bright interior of the building was sliced into individual jewelry stores, or "stalls," as William called them. More than one hundred and twenty, he said, guiding her through the middle aisle. Everywhere she looked there were exquisite gems displayed in glass cases. No, it was not like Covent Garden.

William stopped in front of one of the corner stalls and shook hands with a small elderly man whose expression was serious and respectful. He glanced over at Kate and nodded hello. Kate didn't hear what William said. She was distracted by the rows of sparkling jewels: diamond rings, sapphire earrings, emerald bracelets and ruby necklaces. Diamonds and gold, diamonds and platinum, diamonds combined with other gems and displayed to advantage on black velvet sparkled under the lights.

"Let me take your coat," William offered, sliding it from her shoulders. "It's very warm in here."

"Thank you."

He handed it to the elderly man. "Mind if we leave this with you for a few minutes, Eric?"

"Not at all." The man shot her a questioning look. "May I show you anything, madam?"

"I wish you could." She turned to Will, who looked pleased that she was so impressed. "I've never seen anything like this," she breathed. "Is the whole building full of jewelry?"

"And antique books."

"Good heavens."

"Would you like to look around?"

Look around? She'd like to live here forever. "What about your errand?"

"Eric is taking care of it for me," he assured her. "What period do you like best? Georgian, Victorian or art deco?"

"You explain the difference and I'll decide," she replied, wandering to the next stall. "I never cared for old jewelry until Aunt Belle gave me that brooch."

"GENUINE," the old man whispered reverently. "Absolutely real and of the highest quality. Two of the smaller diamonds are chipped, but that is of no consequence. It needs cleaning, but the large stone is intact. Flawless," he breathed. "Absolutely flawless."

William realized his mouth had dropped open. "You're quite certain?"

Eric looked offended. "I've been studying jewels for forty years, Your Grace. Have you taken it to Longmire's yet? Sheldon will *die* when he sees it. He'll absolutely *die*."

"I feel a little shaky myself," Will said, picking up the coat. "If it was for sale, Eric, what would you expect for it?"

The jeweler turned pale. "I couldn't calculate a value, not until I'd had time to examine all of the stones in the piece. The historical value of such a piece must also be taken into account. The setting is silver gilt, popular in Henry VII's time."

"Not even a guess?" Will urged.

"I wouldn't presume," the little man insisted. "And the young lady? Whatever will she do, walking around with a king's ransom on her lapel?" He lowered his voice to a whisper. "I hope you intend to store it in a vault, Your Grace."

"I intend to take very good care of it," William assured him. "Thank you for your help. And for your discretion."

"I was happy to be able to help such a good customer," Eric said.

William tossed the coat over his arm, then checked to make sure the brooch was still attached to the lapel. The stones were real, which didn't necessarily mean this was the Thorne Diamond, but it certainly meant that Pitty could be on the right track. He would have to tell her she could be right. And he would have to decide how to buy a very expensive piece of family sentiment.

"All set?" Kate approached him and reached for her coat.

"Yes," he said, holding the coat for her. "I suppose I am."

She turned and pulled her hair from the collar. "Is something wrong? You look a little upset."

"Upset?" he echoed. He looked at the pin and tried not to wince. Then he took Kate's hand and moved toward the door. "I'm sure it's nothing a good cup of tea can't cure."

"Before Harrods or after?"

"After," he assured her. He glanced at her shoulder one more time, and the "absolutely real" yellow diamond twinkled at him. What was it worth? A hundred thousand pounds? One million?

Pitty would swoon when she heard the news. Already planning a wedding that would never take place, she'd most likely begin furnishing the nursery for the next Duke.

"Are you sure nothing's wrong?" Kate asked once again.

"Positive," he assured her. They stepped outside into the rainy afternoon, and William fumbled with his umbrella. A feeling of dread settled in his stomach like a lump of cold porridge. Nothing, absolutely nothing and no one could force him into marriage, he promised himself, but the tension in his stomach didn't ease.

"I THINK I'll have to start saving for a silver tea service," Kate declared. She and William sat facing each other in matching wing chairs in front of a cheery fireplace. Between them was a low, polished table filled with a three-tiered serving dish, individual teapots, plates, clotted cream, strawberry jam, sugar, milk and a dish of sliced lemon. "I can't believe how elegant this is."

"I'm glad you're enjoying yourself," the duke replied.

The first tier of the serving dish contained delicate sandwiches. Kate studied the selection, then chose a tiny roll filled with egg salad. "I'm starving. Aren't you?"

"I seem to have lost my appetite today." He selected a watercress sandwich, put it on his plate and poured himself another cup of tea.

A small blob of egg salad landed on the toe of Kate's suede boot. So much for sophistication, she mused, tucking her feet under the table and hoping William hadn't noticed. She wiped her mouth on a pink napkin and looked around the room. Shades of rose and green were in the upholstered furniture and the elaborate printed carpet. They had been seated in a room directly off the lobby, but there were others beyond this one. Couches and chairs were arranged in cozy settings, as if in someone's living room. Every seat was filled. Everyone was drinking tea. It was such a wonderfully *English* setting.

She turned back to William and helped herself to another sandwich. The other tiers contained little cakes and thick scones. She'd take her time and taste everything. "This is a lovely way to end the day."

"Yes." He half smiled. "Very British. Very civilized."

"I'm going to take my time and make this last."

"There is no hurry," he agreed. "No one is waiting for your chair."

"They can't have it." She patted the rose-striped brocade fabric. "I'm going to have to start redoing my apartment."

"When do you return to the States?"

"Tuesday afternoon." She spoke without thinking. "The wedding is Saturday, so by Tuesday Jeff and his new bride will be on their honeymoon. On Wednesday I'll start hunting for a new job."

He frowned. "The wedding?"

"One of the reasons I left the country," she said, picking up her teacup to take a sip. "I couldn't bear to be in town. Saturday was supposed to have been my wedding day, but Jeff is marrying someone else on that day."

"From what you've told me, you're better off without him."

"And you're right." She decided to try a scone. "I realize that now." She thought of her beautiful wedding dress and the four-tiered cake decorated with white roses. Then she thought of Jeff, and the tempting vision of perfect love vanished. "But I'm a slow learner."

"No one can be right all the time. We all make mistakes," he said.

"Even dukes?" she teased, waiting for his answering smile. He didn't disappoint her.

"Oh, *never* dukes." He chuckled. "We're infallible. I'm talking about the common folk."

"Of course you are. You're perfect in every way. Isn't that what your grandmother always told you?"

"As a matter of fact," he drawled, helping himself to a fat scone, "that's precisely what she told me."

"Too bad," Kate replied. "A perfect life doesn't sound very interesting."

"Oh, I don't know. It has its moments." He opened the scone and lathered it with a liberal amount of clotted cream and jam.

Kate copied him and hoped she would like clotted cream. It didn't sound very appetizing, but it looked like whipped butter. She tried a bite, then proceeded to eat the rest. She'd never tasted anything so delicious. "Have you ever been in love?"

He answered without hesitation. "No."

"Never?" She couldn't believe it. "You've never had your heart broken?"

"No."

"You've never written love letters or gotten goose bumps when the phone rang or mooned around listening to romantic music?"

"No."

"That's very strange."

William shrugged. "I don't know why. I've never felt that . . . silly. And I've never felt the need to 'moon around,' as you call it, over Barry Manilow songs. I come from a long line of very unromantic men."

"That's too bad." William Landry would be more interesting if he had a few more flaws.

"Kate, there's something—"

The waiter interrupted by bringing hot water to refresh their tea. "Is everything satisfactory?"

"It was wonderful," Kate assured him.

The duke nodded his approval and asked for the check. When the young man moved to the next table, William set his cup and empty plate on the table. "Kate, there's something you should know—"

"You're really married, with twins?" she joked, trying to forestall what she was afraid might be an embarrassing disclosure. She didn't want to hear an apology for last night's kisses. She didn't want to know that the past days had been some kind of farce. She wanted to return home with only good memories of her trip. She wanted to pretend she'd experienced a little bit of romance with a handsome stranger.

"Very funny."

"Well, I don't think you're gay."

"No." His eyes twinkled as his gaze dropped to her lips. "I don't think so, either."

"You're saying goodbye," she realized, and felt a pang of regret. She would miss him. Which was crazy, because she'd only met him four days ago. She tried to hide her disappointment. "Are you going back to the country now?"

"Shortly," he said, relief evident in his voice. The waiter returned and set the bill, tucked in a leather folder, on the table. Kate made an attempt to take it, but William stopped her. "What are you doing?"

"I wanted to pay this time," she said. "It doesn't seem fair that you are paying for everything. I don't care if you *are* a duke, it's still not fair."

"It is not an issue," he declared, putting a credit card inside the folder. "I am not going to discuss it."

Very haughty, very sweet. "Are you sure?"

He looked at her as if he thought she was insane. "Yes, Kate. I'm positive."

"Then thank you," she said. She bent over and discreetly wiped the egg salad off her boot before she stood up. They collected their coats from the cloakroom, then stepped outside into the misty afternoon.

"Shall we walk?"

"I'd like that." She buttoned her coat and lifted the collar to protect her neck from the chilly wind.

"I wanted—" He stopped, no sound coming out of his mouth.

"Will?"

"The brooch..."

Her hand went to her right lapel but didn't find the familiar stone. She looked down. "It's gone! William, it's gone."

He pulled her under an awning, next to the building. "You had it when we went to Browns. I remember seeing it on your coat when I handed it to the coat-check woman."

"It must have fallen off. It's nothing anyone would want to steal." She felt an embarrassing sting of tears against her eyes. "I'd hate to lose it after all these years."

"Come on. We're not that far away." They hurried back down the sidewalk to the hotel and rushed into the lobby. "Wait here," William ordered.

Kate took a tissue out of her tote bag and wiped her eyes. Will went over to the coat closet and talked to the woman behind the small wooden counter. She let him inside, and they disappeared. Long minutes later he returned, a relieved expression on his face.

"All set," he said when he drew closer. "I have it."

"Thank goodness." Kate held out her hand, and William dropped the brooch into her palm.

"It must have been caught on something, then dropped to the floor when we collected our coats. There doesn't seem to be anything wrong with the clasp, but you should be careful. Perhaps have it checked by a jeweler? I know a good one nearby..."

"I'll have to wait until I get home," she said, placing it carefully in the bottom of her tote.

"Perhaps the hotel safe..."

"I'd rather keep it with me," she told him as they stepped outside once again. She didn't know why, but having the brooch made her feel optimistic. It had brought her luck, in the shape of William Landry. Four days in London had been heaven, and even if she never saw him again, she'd remember.

He walked her into the St. Giles's lobby and took her hand.

"Thank you. For everything," she said.

He looked surprised. "It was my pleasure."

That was that. He smiled, the charming-duke smile she'd grown to expect, then left the hotel. Kate watched him leave, watched his black coat disappear around the corner. He would walk to Essex Court, no doubt. It wasn't that far. Kate swallowed the lump in her throat and tried not to cry. Even the silliest romantic fool wouldn't hope for a kiss goodbye.

6

"I KNEW IT! I knew it all along," Pitty declared, clapping her chubby hands together in delight. "My dear, I cannot tell you how happy I am."

"Don't bother. I can guess," William said, pouring himself a generous helping of unblended Scotch. He took a healthy swallow and allowed himself a satisfied sigh. He didn't know when he'd experienced a day as nerve-racking as this one.

"Well, where is it?"

"I don't have it." He took his drink and sat down in his favorite overstuffed chair. "Do you have the heat on?"

"Yes, but the chill seems to be hanging on." Pitty pushed his feet aside so she could sit on the hassock and face him. Her hot pink sweater made him blink. "Tell me everything," she demanded. "How did you do it?"

"First we toured Kensington Palace." He grimaced. "Kate bought a Duke of Wellington teapot."

"How odd. Were there matching cups?"

"I have no idea." He took another drink and felt his insides begin to warm. "I took her over to Antiquarius. I know one of the dealers and I thought it might be a little less obvious than parading into Longmire's."

"And?"

"Eric said it's the real thing but Sheldon would be the best person to estimate its value."

"Did you make an offer?"

"No. I tried to tell Kate it was valuable, but there were a few, ah, interruptions." Such as losing the damn thing. He could still feel the wave of relief he'd experienced when he'd spotted the pin on the floor behind a fallen coat hanger. He'd held it in his hand, long enough to resist putting it in his pocket. Even though it had been stolen years before, he could not justify its return to the family by illegal means. The stone had been surprisingly warm in his palm.

Pitty gasped. "She doesn't know?" She heaved herself off the hassock and went to the phone. "We must ring her. She can't possibly walk around London wearing something so valuable. What if she loses it before we are able to purchase it?"

"She's not there, Pitty. And she won't lose it," he replied sharply. "It means a great deal to her, too."

"Where is she? We have dinner plans, but perhaps—"

"She's away this evening, Pitty. Something called the Jack the Ripper Tour. And what do you mean, we have 'plans'?"

"Lady Benton, Viscount Lindley and the Smithfields are dining with us tonight."

"Let me guess. Lady Benton is on the list."

"Just a coincidence. I'm feeling particularly social these days, and now Thorne House is almost finished I'm not so tired in the evening."

He leaned back and closed his eyes. There was no way to avoid it. He could no longer use Kate as an excuse to avoid Pitty's social plans. Besides, it would do him good to be with other people for a change. He'd spent the past two evenings with Kate, after all. He thought of the feel of her in his arms and wished she wasn't going on her macabre tour.

"What are you smiling about?"

"Was I smiling?" He opened his eyes to see Pitty close by, peering at him suspiciously.

"You looked positively dreamy," she snapped, frowning. "Not like yourself at all, Willie. Should I worry about you?"

"Of course not."

"What about the brooch?"

"Tomorrow I'll meet with Kate and explain how valuable the brooch is, both monetarily and to our family. We'll go to Longmire's and settle on a price. I'm sure she'll be quite pleased with the amount I'll offer."

"Good, good."

"After that I'm returning to the country. You're welcome to join me if you like. The lambing will be starting soon." He finished his drink and climbed to his feet. It was time to see other women, and it wouldn't hurt to dine with Pitty one more time before he left for the Hall. "I'd better dress for dinner. Is Lady Benton a blonde or brunette?"

KATE REALIZED she'd had too much beer when she had trouble inserting the card in the slot and couldn't open the door to her room. She tried it three more times before the knob finally turned. As she entered her room, she stepped on an envelope that had been slipped under the door.

She opened it and drew out a fax from her sisters. Actually Carol was the one with access to a fax machine, so it must have been her idea. Kate read it quickly. Carol hoped the London tours were working out and she was seeing everything she'd planned; Terri wanted to know if she'd met any interesting men and if she'd packed enough clothes for the English weather; Anne told her not to do anything risky and not go out after dark unless she took a taxi. They wanted her to call them so they would know that she was all right.

Kate decided to put them out of their misery and call. It was five or six hours earlier in Rhode Island, so she tried Anne's number, since she was the one most concerned about safety. The phone only rang twice before Anne's voice said, "Hello?"

"Hi. It's Kate."

"Kate! How are you?"

"I'm fine," she assured her, "but I'm going to keep this really short. I don't want a big hotel bill."

"That's okay. Did you get Carol's fax? Are you having fun?"

"Yes. I just got back from a tour." She didn't specify that it was a spooky tour of Jack the Ripper murder spots that included drinks at three pubs. "How is everyone there?"

"Just fine. We think about you a lot."

Meaning they were worrying. "I'm twenty-five, not seventeen."

"I know. Sometimes it's hard to remember," Anne sighed. "Tell me, have you seen the queen or any royalty yet?"

"Not yet, but there's still hope. I met a duke, though. At Thorne House. Remember I told you I thought we were related to people who once came from Thorne House?"

"Those were just family stories. I think Aunt Belle exaggerated a little. And what do you mean, you met a duke? A *real* duke?"

"The Duke of Thornecrest." Anne clearly didn't believe her.

"Look, sweetie, I bet they *all* say they're dukes. Be careful."

"I will. Don't worry, he's gone to his country estate."

"Sure he has. Don't fall for anything he says. You're vulnerable right now."

For a second Kate didn't know what her sister was talking about. Then she remembered. Jeff's wedding. Her former wedding day. "Anyway, I'm having a great time."

"How old is this supposed duke?"

"In his thirties," Kate fibbed. "And quite handsome. A bachelor, too. I've just left a pub where I was drinking beer with three handsome Germans."

"I should have known you were teasing me," Anne said.

Of course Anne wouldn't believe her. "I'd better go before this costs a fortune. Tell Terri and Carol that I called and that I'm fine. And don't worry. London is beautiful and very safe."

"Take good care," Anne repeated. "And call collect next time."

Kate hung up the phone and kicked off her boots, then hooked her coat behind the door and removed the pin from her black sweater. She'd almost lost it today, but William had found it. It was sweet of him to act as if it was a valuable antique and not a sentimental trinket. She'd miss him. And she'd never forget him—of that she was sure. Even if no one believed her, she'd have photographs to prove he existed. She wished he'd kissed her goodbye, instead of informing her he'd had a "very pleasant day."

Kate hurried to put on her nightgown and get ready for bed. Those mugs of ale had made her tired and maybe even a little bit sad. The Germans had been fun, though. As college students, they'd added a boisterous element to the tour, which had been missing on the trip to Windsor. Two of them had asked her to join them in the hotel's own pub for a nightcap, and she'd thrown caution to the wind and accepted.

She looked at the bags on her bed. She hadn't had time to put today's purchases away before meeting the evening tour group. What on earth was she going to do with a Duke of Wellington teapot?

Remember a duke, of course.

"GO OVER THERE and sit in the lobby," Pitty pleaded. "Katherine has to return to the hotel eventually."

William ignored her. Mary poured him another cup of coffee, and he continued to read the newspaper while his grandmother paced back and forth alongside the dining room table. The IRA had threatened to bomb Heathrow again, and the scandal involving Lord Westley continued. He turned the page, ignored the latest comment on Princess Di's whereabouts and the little princes' school marks.

"You've let her escape," Pitty muttered. "I shall have a stroke before this day is over."

"No, you won't," he said just before his eye was caught by an item in the social column.

Who is the petite redhead dating the D. of T. this week? They've been spotted at the theatre twice, dining cozily at Lorenzo's and snuggling in a taxi. Are L.'s bachelor days numbered?

"Damn," he exclaimed.

Pitty stopped and looked over his shoulder at the newspaper. "Oh. You've finally noticed, have you?"

"What is this rubbish?"

"You can't run about town and not have someone notice."

"Katie's not a redhead," he muttered, tossing the paper on the table.

"*Katie?*" Pitty sniffed. "Are we using *nicknames* now? How cozy."

"Can't a man have a peaceful breakfast without being badgered?"

"Not necessarily," Pitty replied, unruffled by her nephew's temper. She sat down at the table and waved to Mary for more tea. "I think we may have more of a problem than I thought."

"What now, Pitty? I can't imagine what else you want. Aside from my obtaining a priceless brooch, a pin so ugly it boggles the mind. And will shatter my bank account, too."

"I shall buy it myself."

He arched an eyebrow. "And bankrupt yourself?"

"If that's what needs to be done, of course. I can always sell the Monet."

She actually looked sad. William felt guilty. "I apologize," he said, lowering his voice. "I know how important this is to you, but I hope the thing is worth it. It seems a lot of trouble for a—"

"You enjoyed last night?" Pitty interrupted.

"Yes," he lied. He'd have had a better time dining on an airplane.

"Cornelia is lovely."

"Yes." That much was true. She was a little serious for his tastes, but she appeared to be sincere and polite. A little too polite. Boring, almost.

"Will you see her again? I understand her uncle has an estate fifty miles north of the Hall."

"What a coincidence." Kate hadn't told him she was going on a tour today. He wished he could remember the rest of her schedule. There was something about Bath and another day at the museums. He would be very, very careful about explaining why he wanted to buy the brooch. He didn't want her to think he had only been nice to her because he wanted her ugly old pin.

"William!"

He looked over at his grandmother. She was wearing that awful purple robe again. He must remember to purchase a new one for Christmas. Something in white or pale pink. Anything that didn't hurt his eyes in the morning. "What is it now, Pitty?"

"You were daydreaming again." She eyed him curiously. "I'm going into my study. The workmen will be done before noon, and Gregory wants us to accompany him through the renovations to make certain we are pleased."

"Fine. I'll leave a note for Kat—Katherine."

"I can accompany you to her hotel this afternoon."

William nodded. He hadn't committed himself to anything, she noticed. He probably thought he was being sneaky.

Pitty left the room and hurried to her study. There were still ledgers to read, still a mystery to be solved. There had been no mention of Alicia after June of 1814. In fact, there had been few entries in the summer of 1814. Perhaps the duke had been ill during that season, Pitty mused. She took the ledger and sat at her desk, but she didn't open the book.

The third Duke of Thornecrest was the least of her worries. The ninth was giving her fits. Daydreaming, smiling at nothing, following that little American from palace to palace and not complaining. And box seats for *Phantom!* He thought she wouldn't notice such an extravagance? She drummed her fingers on the blotter and looked out the window. The birds would be nesting soon. She would watch their babies hatch and learn to fly.

And Willie, where would he be? Was the brooch already working its magic? If so, she had to get hold of it before her unsuspecting grandson fell in love with the American. He'd been exposed to the yellow diamond for only four days, but she had no idea how long it took to weave its spell. The damage could have been done already, she worried.

After all, the Thorne Diamond was pinned to a totally unsuitable bosom.

"A MESSAGE?"

The woman behind the desk nodded. "If you'll wait a moment, I'll fetch it."

"Thank you," Kate said, wondering who it could be from. William was most likely back "on the farm," and she knew no one else in London. Unless the Germans wanted to party tonight. The serious young woman handed her an envelope, and Kate took it and headed toward the elevator. She'd open it upstairs, after she'd removed her boots.

It had been a wonderful day. Bath was the most romantic place she'd ever seen, Kate decided. She'd spent a lovely hour in the costume rooms, eaten lunch in the famous Pump Room and toured the excavated Roman baths. She'd shopped and walked up hills and down hills. She'd ridden the two-tiered bus from one end of the city to the other. She'd taken a lot of photographs.

She could live there, she decided. Take a "flat" in one of the famous crescents and find a computer job in London. After all, she had a degree in math and four years' experience. And she'd passed a lot of corporate skyscrapers near the airport. The train ride was only seventy minutes from London, but expensive. Maybe she'd be better off living in London and visiting Bath when she felt the need to see rolling hills and Georgian buildings.

The note was brief: "Call me when you return. Yours, William."

Kate sat on the bed and stared at the hotel stationery. It wasn't much of a message, but it made her smile. He hadn't returned to the country after all. He hadn't said goodbye...yet. She reached for the telephone and dialed the numbers printed at the bottom of the page.

The maid answered on the first ring. "Thorne House," she said.

"This is Katherine Stewart, returning William's call," Kate announced, slipping into her "office" voice.

"I'm very sorry, Miss Stewart, but His Grace is not available at the moment. I suggest you call again in the morning."

"Thank you," Kate said, more disappointed than she cared to admit. Maybe he had called to say goodbye after all. Perhaps he had already left for the country. It was after eight. He was most likely at San Lorenzo's, dining with Jessica Somebody and the rest of his aristocratic friends. Kate eased her boots back on and slung her purse over her shoulder. She'd buy a sandwich in the pub downstairs and maybe even have a beer. She would not call him in the morning. It was time to admit they were from two different worlds. It was time to admit there was no reason for a duke to be interested in an unemployed, jilted and slightly depressed computer programmer.

"ARE YOU feeling better, dear?" Pitty looked up from her breakfast as William entered the dining room.

"I'm still a little green around the edges," William answered, "but I'm going to live." He'd been sick most of the night, but he hoped he was over the worst of it.

"Do you think it was something you ate?"

He sat down at the table and poured himself a cup of tea. "I doubt it. I'm afraid it was probably one of the twelve-hour flu bugs."

"I hope so, Willie. You don't look too well."

Since he'd spent half the night hanging over the toilet bowl, the observation didn't surprise him. "I'm feeling much better," he assured her. After several swallows of sweetened tea, he realized the words were true. He was over the worst.

"Good. You'll contact Katherine after breakfast? Or would you prefer I do it?"

William didn't prefer any such thing. "I will take care of it."

"Oh, good. I'm sure Katherine will be quite pleased with her good fortune. She'll be able to buy all the teapots she wants, won't she?"

He didn't pay close attention to what Pitty was chattering about. She wore a silk suit this morning, a bright aqua silk suit with a yellow scarf and pink-and-yellow earrings. She looked like an Easter egg. "You look quite, er, festive this morning. Do you have plans?"

"I'm going to the Fabergé exhibit with Penelope Farley this morning. There's a special showing, then we're off to lunch and a little shopping. Now that the brooch is off my mind, I can concentrate on finding new linens for my bedroom."

"Something bright, I suppose."

"How you do know me," she chirped. "You must tell me Sheldon's reaction when he sees our diamond." She frowned at his paisley robe. "You really shouldn't lounge around any longer, Willie. Once you wash up, you'll feel so much better."

"I think I'll have some toast first," he said. "Or I shall have a relapse and have to spend the rest of the day in bed."

"Don't tease me," she ordered, pushing back her chair. "I'm off!"

William waited until Pitty left before calling Kate. It was almost nine, which was a little late for her, but there was no help for it. He'd overslept. She answered immediately, her voice sounding cautious.

"It's William," he said. "Did you get my message?"

"Yes. I called you last night, but the maid said you were 'unavailable.' I figured you went out."

"No. I was in bed early and didn't want to be disturbed."

"Oh."

He stalled. He didn't want to discuss the brooch over the phone. He wanted to see her again. It could take all day to make the arrangements, but after that he'd be free to leave London and she'd be quite a bit richer for her last days in England. "Where were you off to yesterday?"

"I took the train to Bath."

"Did you enjoy it?" He knew what her answer would be. She'd probably read all of Jane Austen's book and thought the Georgian city was extremely romantic.

"I loved it."

"Meet me in Green Park and tell me all about it. There's something I'd like to show you." He heard the rustle of papers. "What were you planning to see today?"

"Museums."

"The weather is too nice for that. The sun is shining, which means you must walk in the parks. We're quite proud of them, you know." He waited while she considered.

"What time?"

"You decide. I'm still in the middle of breakfast."

She chuckled, her voice sounding sweet and sleepy. "I'm not out of bed, but I'll hurry as fast as I can."

William pictured her curled up in a soft gown, her skin warm and her body waiting for him to slide next to it under the sheets. Now he knew he'd recovered. "Name the time," he managed to say.

"In an hour? I'll get dressed and grab a quick cup of coffee."

"Don't eat too much. We'll go out to lunch. Shall I come to the hotel?"

"Heavens, no. I can find my way around."

"Meet me in front of the Ritz, on Piccadilly. There's a tube station on the corner, if you don't feel like walking."

"Okay. Ten o'clock. The Ritz."

William hung up the telephone and realized he hadn't told her to wear the brooch. In fact, he'd forgotten all about it.

That was not a good sign.

IT WAS FOOLISH to be so happy to see him again. He looked a little pale, and there were shadows under his eyes, as if he hadn't slept well. But he smiled when he saw her, and Kate smiled in return. She didn't like thinking that she'd missed his company yesterday, but it was true.

"I see you still have the brooch," he said.

"I'm taking good care of it," she assured him. The brooch was securely fastened to her black sweater. She'd left her coat in her room and figured she'd be warm enough without it. "I felt awful when I lost it the other day."

"So did I," he said, and she had the strange feeling he meant it. "Let's walk through here." He led her along a path toward Buckingham Palace. "Look," he said, pointing to their left. "The tan roof is Thorne House."

"I didn't know it was this close to Green Park."

"Yes. That's the view from the rooms in the back, in the museum."

"How is the refurbishment coming along?"

"It's almost done. The dust covers will come off, and the house will be cleaned for the tourist season. Pitty is pleased."

"I can imagine." Kate felt at home as they strolled through the park, then watched the Queen's Guards ride their horses along the horse path in Hyde Park. They stopped to catch the Changing of the Guard at Buckingham Palace, then walked back toward Piccadilly and the bustling sidewalks.

"How about lunch at the Ritz?"

"Really? Am I dressed for it?" She frowned at her calf-length brown skirt and matching suede boots. "Is this appropriate for a place like the Ritz?"

"You're perfect." He meant it. He thought he was crazy for meaning it. He took her elbow and led her into the elegant hotel. "Don't worry. You'll be treated like a queen. And if you're lucky, we may even find a gift shop."

He requested a table overlooking the park. The majordomo recognized him and gave William what he wanted. They treated her like . . . a duchess, Kate decided. And she liked it. She hoped the afternoon would last a long time. It wasn't every day she was bowed to every time someone refilled her wineglass.

"There is a favor I need to ask you," William began when they had finished their lunch. "It's rather strange, but I hope you won't mind."

"Ask me anything."

"It's about the brooch," he said. "It's quite valuable, Kate. In fact, it's a priceless example of medieval jewelry. It used to belong in my family, and I'd like to purchase it."

She touched the yellow stone. "You're talking about *this* brooch?"

"The center stone is a six-carat canary diamond. It's really quite rare."

"*This* brooch?"

He nodded. "Pitty recognized it immediately as a piece that had belonged to the first Duchess of Thornecrest. It, ah, disappeared in the early 1800s. Presumed stolen, you see."

"But it's been in my family for years. How could it be—" She stopped. "You think someone in my family stole it from someone in your family?"

"I have no idea."

"Maybe there are two. Yours and mine."

"Not with a stone like that. You have to admit, the brooch is really quite, ah, original."

"Meaning gaudy."

"I'm not debating the quality of the design, Kate." He really didn't want to debate anything. He wanted to get this whole thing over with so he could return to the country where it was quiet and sane.

"I don't believe this." She finished her wine in one large gulp. "I know I've believed a lot of weird things in my life, but this isn't going to be one of them. Thank you for lunch."

"Kate." He put his hand on her arm. She looked as if she was getting ready to bolt. "I can prove it."

"How?"

"We will go to a jeweler near here. Very reliable, of course. They deal in only the finest gems and are also experts in antique jewelry. They will be able to tell if the brooch is authentic and how much I should pay for it."

"Could I have some more wine?" she asked in a small voice. "I don't usually drink, but this is a special occasion."

He smiled, satisfied that the afternoon was going so well. "You're about to become a very wealthy woman, I fear."

Kate looked at him, her eyes wide. The waiter refilled her glass and, sensing drama, quickly left. "Oh, I have no intention of selling it."

William's smile faded. He couldn't believe what he thought she'd said. "Pardon?"

"I'm not going to sell a family heirloom. It wouldn't be right."

"Why not? You can buy something else."

"I'm to hand it down to my daughters. Someday I'll get married and have children."

It was time to change tactics. "It's going to cost you a small fortune to insure it. You're going to have to keep it in a vault."

"That's if I believed you. I get the feeling that there's more to this than you've told me. Maybe you're a jewel thief or a smuggler."

"I'm a *farmer*," he sputtered. "I make cheese."

"Cheese?"

"Cheese." William motioned the waiter for the check and quickly paid the bill. "Jewel thieves don't own dairy farms."

Kate felt a little dizzy. She wondered if she should leave the elegant dining room and disappear into the bustling city. This is when her sisters would say, "Get out. You don't really believe all this, do you?"

She touched the sparkling stone, remembering the way the waiter's eyes had widened when he saw it. And the curious expression on the antique dealer's face yesterday. She turned to William as they walked across the crowded dining room. "You took me to Antiquarius on purpose, didn't you? You took my coat and handed it to that little man and let me wander off while he examined it, didn't you?"

He sighed. "Yes."

She shook her head in disbelief. "This is amazing, absolutely amazing."

"My sentiments exactly," William muttered, following her through the door. "Shall we?" He motioned toward the crosswalk. "Longmire's is in this direction. Don't you want to know what that pin is worth? Aren't you the least bit curious?"

Kate took a deep breath of fresh air and slipped on her sunglasses. "I'm a *lot* curious, but that doesn't mean I'm going to sell it to you."

"Let's discuss that after the appraisal."

She walked beside him in silence, but her mind was churning with questions. The first day in London his grandmother had stared at the brooch and had asked her about its origins. And ever since, her grandson had escorted an American tourist around the city. He'd wanted to buy it; he'd wanted it appraised.

7

"NOW WHAT?"

"Tea." He took her elbow and guided her toward St. James Street. "You look a little pale."

"I'm wearing a quarter of a million pounds on my chest," Kate said. She could still see the look of shock on the jeweler's face when she'd handed him the brooch. "I guess that could be making me a little shaky. Where are we going?"

"Home," he answered, and began to hurry her across the street when the signal turned green. "We'll get some tea into you and go on from there."

Kate stayed close to him but didn't reply. This was no time to tell him there would be no "going on." The handsome duke thought all he had to do was write a check and she'd hand over her one and only family heirloom. She had no fiancé and no job, but she sure as hell had Aunt Laurabelle's prized possession, and no one was going to take it from her. Besides, Aunt Belle had promised that the brooch would bring her heart's desire. Kate was determined to keep it, at least until her "heart's desire" arrived.

They were inside Thorne House in a matter of minutes, and Kate barely had time to admire the hall before Will swept her past the cleaning crew, into the elevator and up to the third floor.

"Mary!" he called as he led Kate through the foyer and into the living room. When the maid appeared in the doorway, William ordered tea, then turned to Kate. "Are you feeling faint?"

"No," she lied. Actually she was feeling a little woozy, but she didn't want William to know. She sank into one of the wing chairs and touched the brooch to make sure it was still there. She'd insisted on wearing it when they left the store, despite disapproving looks from the jeweler and his young assistant. She'd wanted to walk out of that fancy store the same way she'd come in—wearing her twelve-dollar dangle earrings and her worth-a-fortune diamond brooch.

Mary appeared holding a heavy tray piled with all the necessary ingredients for tea and placed it on a low table by Kate's knees. William thanked her and shooed her out of the room. Kate didn't know if she could say a word. She leaned back and closed her eyes while William fiddled with the teapot.

"Drink this," he said, and she opened her eyes and took the delicate cup and saucer from his hand.

"Thanks," she said, and took a sip. "You're right. Tea was just what I needed."

"You're becoming quite an Englishwoman."

"It's the black clothes."

"What?"

"Never mind." She watched him sit down. He seemed to have forgotten to pour himself anything.

He leaned forward and clasped his hands together. "When are you leaving London?"

Leaving London was not what she wanted to discuss. "Tuesday afternoon."

"That gives me time."

"For what?"

He didn't answer. Instead, he stood and walked over to the sideboard and poured himself a drink. "I have to return to Leicestershire, but I can arrange with the bank to pay the sum you require for the brooch. By Monday that should be accomplished."

"But I'm not going to sell it."

His eyebrows rose. "Do you think that's wise?"

"I'm not famous for making smart decisions," she said, "but I don't think *anyone* would believe this particular story, do you?" She might never tell her sisters about this, she decided. They'd lock her up.

"You still don't believe the stone is genuine?"

"I've seen enough movies to make me wonder if I'm in the middle of a sting."

He choked back a laugh. "A sting," he repeated. "You think I could be trying to con you?" She nodded, and he couldn't help chuckling. "And you don't believe I'm a duke, either, I assume."

She studied him as he crossed the room and sat in the chair near her. Expensive haircut, expensive clothes and accessibility to Thorne House. William Landry had a sophisticated presence that broadcast an aristocratic upbringing. All signs pointed to the fact that he was who he said he was. "No," she replied. "I guess I believe you're a duke."

"Who else would he be, my dear?" Pitty, elegant and cheerful in a bright aqua suit, swept into the room and patted William's cheek before she sat down on the couch. "Tea! Perfect." Mary brought another cup and saucer and set them in front of the duchess.

"Thank you," the dowager said, obviously pleased with something. She smiled at Kate and William. "What have you two been up to this afternoon?"

William answered. "We've been to Longmire's, Pitty. Sheldon wished for more time to appraise the stones, but he evaluated the piece at a quarter of a million pounds."

"Oh, my," Pitty breathed, forgetting to pour herself any tea. "So, he thought it was the Thorne Diamond?"

"Yes."

She turned to Kate. "What a lovely surprise for you!"

Kate wasn't sure if that statement required an answer. Being told the brooch was valuable was one thing; believing it was another. "Yes, I guess you could say that."

Pitty's gaze dropped to the pin. "Magnificent." She looked at Kate and smiled. "It's been lost for five generations. I suppose William told you it, ah, disappeared in the early 1800s."

Kate set her empty cup on the table. "He also told me that means one of my ancestors stole it."

Pitty nodded. "Yes, that's highly probable. More tea?"

"No, thank you." She wanted to leave this mansion and its crazy rich inhabitants and go back to her tiny hotel room and collapse. She wanted to put her brooch in the little safe at the bottom of the armoire and then she wanted to take a nap. "My great-great-whatever-aunt or grandmother did not steal anything."

"How else would it have appeared in America?" Pitty asked as she poured herself a cup of tea. "I've been reading through the family journals. No mention is made of a relative emigrating to America in that particular century. There are no records of Landry daughters, not since 1653. William, go through the books in the Hall library and see if there are any more journals there. We should be able to find something that solves this mystery."

Kate touched the brooch again, just to remind herself it was still there. She had a feeling she'd be doing that a lot from now on. "My ancestors aren't jewel thieves."

Pitty's three chins quivered. "My dear, I mean no offense, but one cannot rewrite history."

William shot Kate an unexpectedly sympathetic smile. "You don't have to decide anything right away," he said. "There is no rush."

"No rush?" Pitty yelped. Drops of tea spattered from her cup and spotted her wide aqua bosom. "After one-hundred and eighty years there's *no rush*? Willie, for heaven's sake!"

"A few days aren't going to make any difference either way, Pitty. I'm leaving for the country this evening, as planned. I'll be happy to make all the arrangements with the bank—"

Pitty's teacup clattered to the table. "No!" She took a deep breath and fanned herself with her hand before turning to Kate. "You will go to Thorne Hall with William and see the picture of the first duchess wearing *that* brooch. Then you will believe me when I say you are wearing the Thorne Diamond, the diamond that belongs in my family, where it should have been all these years."

Kate protested. Spend the night under the same roof with a man who made her heart pound when he looked at her? A man who kissed with amazing passion and left her breathless? She struggled to come up with an excuse. "I can't leave London. I'm staying at the St. Giles. I'm supposed to be going to Westminster Abbey tomorrow afternoon. In the morning I'd planned to do a gravestone rubbing at St. Martin's—"

"There are graves at Thorne Hall," Pitty interrupted. "Plenty of them. Rub all the stones you want, but first—"

"That's enough, Pitty," William said, a thread of steel running through his voice.

His grandmother stopped in midsentence. "William?"

"You are not going to bully Kate any longer." He turned to Kate and lowered his voice. "Would you like me to escort you to the St. Giles now?"

"Yes. Just call a cab." The long days of touring had finally caught up with her, she realized. She needed some quiet time to absorb everything that had happened.

He turned back to his grandmother. "I'm going to send for my car. I packed this morning, so I'll drop Kate at her hotel and head north."

"William . . ."

Will ignored her, moved to the phone in the corner of the room and spoke a few words into the receiver. When he was finished he excused himself. "I'm going to fetch my things. Not one more word to Kate about the brooch," he warned, giving Pitty a sharp look. "She's been through quite enough for one day, and so have I."

Pitty hesitated, but William didn't move until he had her consent. When he'd left the room, the elderly woman leaned back against the couch cushions and sighed loudly. "I'm too old for this kind of excitement," she said.

"I know what you mean," Kate agreed. They sat in silence for a long moment until Pitty sighed again.

"I only want what's best for him," she muttered. She turned faded blue eyes toward Kate. "He's all I have."

Kate wasn't sure what to say, but the duchess didn't seem to expect a response.

"His grandfather was completely worthless. I don't know why I ever married him. His father—my son—was a sweet boy, but married a woman totally wrong for him. I told him, but would he listen to me? Of course not. Willie is a fine boy, smart and sensitive, but much too stubborn." She studied Kate with an assessing eye. "Have you ever been married?"

"No. I was supposed to have been married tomorrow," Kate replied.

"Tomorrow? What happened?"

"He said I wasn't—" she didn't want to say *desirable* to the Duchess "—interesting enough. He found someone else and is marrying her tomorrow instead."

"How very fascinating," the duchess said, leaning forward. "And were you quite devastated?"

"At first," Kate admitted. "And then I realized he probably wasn't the right man for me after all. I wanted to be married and have children. More than I wanted to marry Jeff, I think."

"Having children is very important," the duchess agreed, her expression thoughtful. She struggled to rise from the couch, then perched on the chair next to Kate's and patted her hand. "My dear, I am going to give you some advice and I'd like you to listen very carefully."

Kate waited, wondering what on earth was coming next. For some odd reason, despite the fact that the old woman thought one of her ancestors had stolen jewelry for a living, she liked William's grandmother. The mischievous light in the faded blue eyes reminded her of Aunt Belle. Kate found herself willing to hear the dowager's words. "All right," she agreed.

"Go to the Hall with him. Just for two days. You'll have a lovely time seeing the Midlands. It's a large house, with a small staff. You would be quite comfortable."

"It sounds lovely," Kate said. "But—"

"The painting is above the fireplace in the formal dining room," Pitty explained. "The first duchess was a beautiful woman, very much in love with her husband."

"I'm sure she—"

Pitty continued as if she didn't hear her. "You shouldn't be alone on the day you were to be married, do you think?"

"I don't—"

Pitty tugged on her hand. "Is it such a difficult decision? A day in the country with a handsome devil like my William?"

The handsome devil himself stepped into the room and dropped his bags in the wide doorway. "We're ready," he announced. He looked like a man ready to flee prison. "Kate?"

She stood, and the dowager did also. Kate held out her hand, and the old woman took it, but didn't let it go. "I enjoyed meeting you," Kate said, meaning the words. "I don't intend to sell the brooch, so I don't think we'll see each other again."

"One never knows," Pitty murmured. She looked at Will, standing stubbornly in the door, and raised her voice. "I have done my best to convince Kate to see the portrait at the Hall."

William stared at his grandmother. "What's going on?"

"Kate shouldn't be alone tomorrow." She patted Kate's arm. "Right, my dear?"

Kate took a deep breath. She'd come to England to see things she'd never seen before, to have an adventure and forget about her nonexistent career and her canceled wedding. She told herself that her acceptance of Pitty's invitation wasn't because going to Thorne Hall meant she would have another day with William. "I'd like to see the portrait, if you don't mind my tagging along."

"We'll stop at the hotel for your things. You'll be spending the night." No "how wonderful," no smile of pleasure or sigh of relief. Kate felt like an idiot for expecting a reaction from him.

"Thank you," the dowager whispered, squeezing Kate's hand. "Wear the brooch all the time so you don't lose it," she advised. "We'll discuss its future ownership on Monday."

"But—"

"Go," Pitty said. "Have a lovely weekend, children."

William kissed her on the cheek and picked up his bags. Kate followed him into the brass-trimmed elevator. Five days ago she wouldn't get into a cab with him. Now she was heading off to the country in his car.

It boiled down to one thing, she realized, following the silent man outside to the waiting Jaguar sedan.

She wasn't ready to say goodbye.

PITTY HAD SOMETHING up her sleeve. He could tell by the innocent expression in her eyes when she'd said goodbye. William nearly groaned out loud as he waited in his car for Kate to reappear with her luggage. This was insane. He could barely keep his hands off her in taxicabs and now he was taking her to his home.

He wanted to spend the weekend making love to her. He wanted those soft breasts in his palms and that sweet little body pressed against his. He wanted to bury himself inside her and watch her eyes darken with passion.

And he couldn't. A weekend affair would only be messy. One night, he promised himself. One night and a tour of the manor house. The dairies, too, if she wanted to photograph British cows. She could gaze up at a hundred paintings of dead Landrys for as many hours as she liked, then he would bring her back to London and say goodbye. He would turn right around and go back to Leicestershire. To mud, cows, dogs, sheep and all the rest, and he would heave a sigh of relief to have escaped yet another romantic entanglement.

William drummed his fingers on the steering wheel and wondered why the prospect of saying goodbye to Katie Stewart made his stomach knot up. Making love to her held much more appeal. He hardened his heart as Kate hurried from the hotel and crossed the sidewalk, a carry-on bag slung over her shoulder and the familiar tote bag in her hand. She opened the back door and tossed her bags in as William leaned over to open the passenger's door.

Once she was inside, seat belt fastened and sunglasses in place, Kate gave him a big smile. "I wasn't sure this was the right thing to do," she said, "but I couldn't resist seeing more of England."

He drove carefully into the late-afternoon traffic. "Why wasn't it the right thing to do?"

"You didn't invite me. Your grandmother did. You were forced into going along with it."

William glanced at her when he stopped the car for a red light. "I rarely allow myself to be forced into anything." *Except following a tourist to the Tower of London and playing tour guide for a week.*

"Really?"

He'd always been a sucker for green eyes. "Really." He put the car in gear and headed north. Keeping his mind off sex wasn't going to be easy.

KATE DIDN'T INTEND to fall asleep. Leicestershire was one hundred miles north of London, William had explained, punching the radio buttons until he found classical music. One hundred miles was a long time to listen to Beethoven and struggle to keep her eyes open, so she curled up on the soft ivory leather and rested her head against the back of the seat. When she woke, it was dark and the car had slowed down.

She opened her eyes and straightened up. "Where are we?"

"Northeast of Leicestershire, near Rutland."

The directions meant nothing. "Are we close?"

"Very. We've been driving through Thornecrest land for over a mile." He pointed to a road leading through green pastures to a prosperous-looking farmstead. "One of my dairies."

"One? How many are there?"

"Five," he said, pride tingeing his voice. "We're one of the biggest dairy operations in the Midlands."

"That must be a lot of milk."

"We use it," William said. He pointed ahead. "There. See the stone pillars?"

She could barely make out the markers through the dark. "Yes. What are they?"

"The entrance to Thorne Hall." He turned the car left and swung onto a wide paved road. Kate expected to see a house, but the surrounding fields were dark. Trees lined the road and low hills rolled to the horizon.

"Where's the Hall?"

"You should be able to see it soon." They crested a small hill, and in the distance, lights spilled out of the windows of an immense stone building. "There." Will stepped on the gas pedal and hurried along the road, which eventually curved in front of the stone mansion.

Kate couldn't think of anything to say. Grander and more impressive than she'd ever imagined, Thorne Hall faced acres of manicured lawns. Trees rose from either side of the three-story building, an arched entrance protected the door and ivy occupied much of the space between the mullioned windows.

"It was built in 1695," William explained. "But two-thirds of the house was destroyed in the early 1800s. It's a manageable size now."

"It's beautiful." Kate tried to picture a structure three times its size, but couldn't. William parked the car in front of the entrance and stepped out of the car, as did

Kate. A round-faced older gentleman scurried from the front door and down the steps.

"Welcome home, sir!"

"Thank you, Harry. It's good to be home." William turned to Kate. "I'd like you to meet my guest, Katherine Stewart. Kate, this is Harry Goodfellow. He and his wife run Thorne Hall."

"Welcome to Thorne Hall, Miss Stewart." Harry hurried past them to the car.

"Thank you." She was in heaven, all right. Kate let William lead her up the wide stone steps to a massive door. He opened it and ushered her into the hall. The "great hall," William called it and led the way, explaining a bit about the architecture. Kate tried not to let her mouth hang open as she walked across a black-and-white marble floor. Pale stone walls rose for two stories, and a wide stone staircase swept to an upper balcony. Portraits hung everywhere, and over the doors and the fireplace were ornate carvings of fruit and cherubs.

"On the right is the formal dining room and, beyond that, the morning room." William waved toward a double door opened to reveal yellow walls. "Straight ahead is the main salon and Long Gallery. To the left are the library and offices." He looked down and smiled at her. "Don't look so worried. You won't get lost. The house was redesigned in 1949, after World War II, so it would be economical and efficient."

"I feel as if I'm back in another century." Rhode Island was very far away, another lifetime even. An unemployed computer programmer didn't expect to be standing beside a duke beneath carved cupids.

The feeling of unreality continued as William led her up the stone staircase, past pictures of his ancestors painted with their horses, dogs or armor. A few looked pleasant enough, but most appeared as if they took their titles seriously. The upper floor was split into east and west wings. William led her to the west, explaining the east-wing rooms were only used when Pitty visited or there was a large house party over the holidays.

"How many rooms are there up here?"

"Ten." He led her down a long hall, its wall painted soft ivory. A pale green-and-yellow floral carpet softened their footsteps. "My rooms are at the end of the hall." He opened the first door on the right. "This is the largest guest room, Kate, so you should be comfortable enough." He flicked the light switch, and a tiny bedside lamp lit the room.

"I think it's perfect," she managed to say as she stepped inside the room. Ivory walls and yellow carpet gave the large room a sunbathed glow. Lace curtains hung from the tall windows at either side of the double bed, and a matching lace coverlet decorated the bed. It was an exquisitely furnished room, fit for a queen, Kate thought. Harry arrived with her bags and set them down on the floor by a chintz-covered chaise lounge.

"If you need anything, just ring for Mrs. Goodfellow." William pointed to a set of buttons in the wall beside the bed. He looked at his watch. "It's almost eight. I'll check with her to find out about dinner, but I suspect it's ready when we are. Are you starving or would you like a chance to freshen up?"

"Give me ten minutes," Kate said. Ten minutes to convince herself she wasn't dreaming. Trite but highly necessary. Especially when she looked at the Manet hanging over the cherry bed.

"I'll knock," he promised, and followed Henry out of the room. William paused in the doorway and looked back at Kate. "You're not afraid of dogs, are you?"

"Not usually."

"Good." He shut the door behind him and left her alone in the elegant yellow room. Along one wall were three doors: one was the entrance to a large white-and-gold bathroom, the others, on either side of the bathroom, opened on empty closets. Kate's clothes did little to fill the closet on the right. She splashed cold water on her face, redid her makeup and willed her queasy stomach to behave. It was nerves, she decided. She'd been on edge since the visit to Longmire's.

This morning she'd awakened planning to visit the Victoria and Albert Museum. Tonight she wore a priceless diamond and would sleep in Thorne Hall under a Manet. Kate took several deep breaths. No wonder she was a little unsettled.

She sat on the edge of the bed and rubbed her forehead. Her real problem wasn't owning a brooch worth almost four hundred thousand dollars, or being a guest in a mansion three hundred years old. Her real problem was being perilously close to falling in love with William Landry. If she wasn't already. She could leave here tomorrow with her pride intact. He would never have to guess an awestruck American tourist had fallen for him if she was very, very careful. She would be cool and sophisticated. She would enjoy her tour of the country and admire the portrait of that duchess with the brooch. She would return to London tomorrow, maybe by train.

No one would ever have to know she'd spent her London vacation falling in love with a duke.

It was so ridiculous that no one would believe it anyway.

MRS. GOODFELLOW LIKED HER. William could tell by the way the plump woman bustled around Kate's chair and served her healthy portions of roast beef and Yorkshire pudding. Harry had winked at him in the hallway, showing his silent approval of the surprise house guest. The pair of springer spaniels tried to lick her hand and whined for attention, while the tiny mutt Mrs. Goodfellow had rescued last summer wagged her tail and put her tiny brown paws on the seat of Kate's chair until Henry called the dogs from the dining room.

Kate didn't appear to mind the dog's attention, William thought. In fact, she seemed oblivious to the commotion her presence at Thorne Hall had caused. Mrs. Goodfellow had dragged out the finest plates and had filled a silver vase with daffodils as if the queen herself was to eat in the dining room Henry Holland had designed in 1788. In fact, silver gleamed everywhere. Kate was seated to his left, beyond a trio of candles in an arrangement of silver candlestick holders.

The platter of beef almost crashed to the floor when Mrs. Goodfellow spotted the brooch on Kate's sweater.

William hurried to lend a hand and avoid giving the dogs the meal of a lifetime. "There," he said, steadying the gleaming silver platter.

"Thank you," Mrs. Goodfellow murmured. As she met Will's gaze, her eyebrows rose as if to say "What on earth is going on here, Willie?"

He pretended he didn't notice. "Everything looks wonderful. You've outdone yourself."

"Your grandmother called. Said you were bringing a special guest." She moved away from the table. She smiled once more at Kate. "Wanted everything to be lovely."

"It is," Kate assured her, and moved her fork around on her plate as if to prove her words. When Mrs. Goodfellow had left them alone in the room, she glanced up at the portrait above the fireplace. "I guess that proves it, doesn't it?"

"Proves what?"

"The brooch belonged to your family."

"Hard to imagine there would be two pieces of jewelry that looked like that, isn't it?" The first duchess wore a flowing white gown, with the ornate brooch pinned to her ample bosom. A crown of flowers topped her dark curls, and her smile was kind. William had never minded having her in the dining room.

"Yes. Are you sure there wasn't a Landry woman who went to the United States? Maybe she owned the brooch and it was hers to take with her."

William shrugged. "I doubt it. Pitty wondered the same thing and has been going through old journals from the nineteenth century. Have you forgiven me yet?"

"For which offense?"

He couldn't tell if she was teasing him or not. "How many are there?"

"Deceiving me at the tower, hiding the fact that the brooch was valuable, pretending you were taking me out because you wanted to and—"

"I apologize. I was speaking of today. I know it's been a shock for you."

Kate nodded toward the portrait. "You're forgiven. I'm starting to understand why your grandmother wanted me to see that. The brooch belongs to a duchess obviously."

"Aren't you hungry?"

"Not very." She put down her fork and dabbed her lips with her napkin. "I don't want to hurt Mrs. Goodfellow's feelings."

"You won't. I'll eat enough for both of us tonight."

"All right." Kate looked at him gratefully. "It was kind of you to bring me here. I'll take the train back to London tomorrow. There is a train station in Leicestershire, isn't there?"

William deliberately looked at his plate and cut a piece of beef. "Yes, but you're welcome to stay the weekend."

"I don't think so. There's still a lot I want to—"

"Of course," he agreed a little too quickly. "I'll show you the dairies in the morning if you like."

"I'd like that." Her eyes sparkled in the candlelight, but her skin was pale, making her look fragile and vulnerable.

"Was tomorrow really to have been your wedding day?"

"Yes. Up until three weeks ago." She smiled at him. "Don't look so sorry for me. I'm not."

"No?" He put down his fork and reached for her hand. He told himself it was a friendly and sympathetic gesture that meant nothing. Heat snaked through his fingers and up his arm and knocked him in the groin.

She squeezed his fingers gently, then pulled her hand away.

"Don't go," he whispered.

"I have to." She gulped, scooting her chair away from the table. "Excuse me."

"Don't go." He stood and reached for her, but she shook her head. Her face was very white. "Stay and—"

"I can't," she insisted. "I'm not feeling—"

Too late he realized every bit of color had drained from her face. He reached for her and caught her in his arms before she crumpled to the floor.

8

"I'M SO EMBARRASSED," Kate moaned. "Go away."

"No." William held a cold cloth to her forehead.
"This is all my fault."

"How? Did you poison me?" Kate kept her eyes
closed and tried to ignore the queasy feeling that rolled
in waves throughout her body. Vomiting was bad
enough. Vomiting all over the Duke of Thornecrest was
a disaster.

He chuckled softly. "No. But I had this flu yesterday.
I was sick as a dog, too, for about twelve hours. I must
have given it to you."

"I'm never kissing you again," she moaned.

"You're breaking my heart," he whispered. "Lie still
and try to relax."

"What time is it?"

"Almost three. You should be able to sleep soon."

Sleep or kill herself, Kate decided. Will had helped
her back and forth to the bathroom, and when she was
too weak to get out of bed, he'd held a basin and rubbed
her back. Will stroked the damp cloth across her forehead and down the side of her face. "Mmm," she said.
"Feels good."

"Go to sleep."

"You, too."

"When you're better," he said, his voice low and
soothing.

"I'm better," she whispered, but she kept her eyes closed. She'd moved past embarrassment, she realized. Past embarrassment and into total humiliation. Tomorrow she'd crawl out of here and hitch a ride to the train station. She wouldn't have to face him and she would never tell anyone what had occurred during her visit to a country estate.

"Go to sleep," he repeated. "I'll leave when I'm sure you're going to be all right. I don't want you fainting on my marble floors and breaking any bones."

"You'd be stuck with me forever," she sighed. "Not good."

There was a brief silence. "That's a matter of opinion, isn't it?"

Kate didn't answer. She turned onto her side and slipped into a welcome sleep. William watched her for a while until he was satisfied that the worst was over. He left a light burning in the bathroom and made sure Kate was covered with a blanket before he tiptoed out of the room. He'd never been good at taking care of anyone. In fact, he couldn't remember ever having done it before tonight. There were no younger brothers and sisters, no cousins or nieces and nephews. But he thought he'd done pretty well. After all, what choice had he had after she collapsed?

If he hadn't been through the same thing the night before, he would have panicked and called a physician. He still would, William promised himself, if Kate hadn't improved by morning. He went through his sitting room and on to his bathroom. He'd take a shower and go to bed, but he'd leave his door open in case Katie needed him.

SUNLIGHT WAS POURING in through the lace when Kate opened her eyes. She was going to live. The queasiness was gone; the wanting-to-die feeling was gone, too. Kate tried to sit up and was glad when no dizziness interrupted the motion. She saw her reflection in the mirror over the antique makeup table: tangled hair, pale skin and dark circles under her eyes that made her look as if she'd escaped from a mental institution. She'd vomited in front of a duke. She'd vomited *on* a duke. She'd been sick all over someone she was half in love with. Talk about killing passion.

And, even worse, today was to have been her wedding day. Kate put her head in her hands and groaned.

"Miss?" Mrs. Goodfellow paused in the doorway. "I brought you some tea. His Grace thought you might be needin' some nourishment."

"He's not around, is he?"

"No. He's outside, but he'll be back in a while." She set the tray on a little glass-topped table in the corner. "You'll have time to freshen up."

"Thank goodness."

She poured a cup of tea. "What do you take in your tea?"

"Just a little sugar, but you don't have to wait on me."

"No." Mrs. Goodfellow stopped her with one chubby hand. "You stay right where you are. It's not often we have guests. Are you feeling better? I hear you had a nasty case of flu."

Kate took the teacup and sipped. The hot, sweet liquid was just what she needed. "I'm fine. A little shaky, but nothing worse."

"Good, good. There's some toast and a few biscuits, too. And my own strawberry jam."

"Thank you very much, for everything. I'm not used to being waited on."

"We've our orders to give you the royal treatment." Mrs. Goodfellow winked at her. "Wouldn't do to have Will, er, His Grace, think we didn't do what we were told."

"Have you worked here long?"

"All my life. My husband, too. And my mother before that."

"Then you've known Will all his life."

"A fine boy." Mrs. Goodfellow nodded. She handed Kate a plate of toast. "Take a bite of that and see how you go along."

"All right." Kate tasted the fresh-baked toasted bread and smiled. "Heaven," she declared. "I must be better if I'm hungry."

"Yes," the plump housekeeper declared, "that's the truth of it, all right. You'll need to build your strength up if you're going to see Thorne Hall and all that it entails. The dairies alone will take hours."

"Are there that many cows?"

"Oh, yes, but the cheese is the most interestin', I think, though not like they made it in my grandmother's day. You'll be getting a real treat. Finish your toast so you can pop into the bath before he returns."

"Good idea."

"Don't worry about the tray," Mrs. Goodfellow said. "I'll send one of the girls for it later." She closed the door behind her, leaving Kate to wonder how long it was going to take to look halfway decent. She was determined to succeed or die trying.

"HOW ARE YOU FEELING?" William crossed the stone floor and stopped at the bottom of the staircase. He watched Kate hesitate for a second, then continue down the stairs toward him. She looked fragile in a black sweater and brown leggings. The brooch peeked out from beneath the collar of a white shirt and the rounded neck of the sweater. He was getting accustomed to having the damn thing in his face all the time.

"Much better, thank you."

She still looked embarrassed. He wanted to put his arms around her to reassure her, the way he had last night. He'd sat on the mattress next to her, and she'd melted into his arms and he'd felt very strong and protective. "You look fine."

Kate joined him at the base of the stairs. "I'm feeling much better." Her smile was rueful. "Thanks for taking care of me last night. I didn't mean to fall into your arms quite so dramatically."

"That was the best part. I'm sure my ancestors saw a lot of swooning women, but I never have."

"You knew what to do."

"Genetic memory." There, he'd managed to make her smile, a real smile, which made him feel ten feet tall. "Are you ready for a tour or would you prefer to relax in the library?"

"A tour, I think. Fresh air would feel good."

"All right. It's a bit breezy and damp, but the sun is trying to come out. Maybe we'll be lucky." He led her to a narrow hall behind the dining room that took them past an enormous kitchen and into a warren of smaller rooms.

"You'll need this." William tossed her a heavy leather jacket lined in shearling. "You're going to need some protection from the wind." He rummaged through the collection of boots lined up under the coat rack until he found a small pair of waterproof boots. "These, too," he said, and handed them to her. "Do you want to see the gardens or something muddier?"

"Both, as long as I'm outside." She kicked her shoes off and stuck her feet in the boots. "Hey, that's a pretty good fit."

"Good."

She pulled a pair of old work gloves from the pocket of the coat. "Mind if I wear these, too?"

"Go ahead." He smiled. She looked cute in the over-size coat. "You look a lot better than you did last night."

She shuddered. "Don't remind me."

"Come on." He held out his gloved hand and she took it. "You might as well see how a duke spends his time."

Kate grinned up at him, her eyes twinkling. "You mean you *work?*"

He tugged her closer and gave her a quick, hard kiss on those inviting lips. He purposely didn't linger, or he knew he'd be making love to her in spite of mud-caked boots and old jackets. He lifted his head and tugged her toward the door. There was a new intimacy between them this morning. After all, he'd held her in his arms half the night.

William took a deep breath of fresh air and promised himself he could make it through the morning, get Kate on a train, and ignore the aching in his gut.

THE BRIEF KISS CAUGHT Kate by surprise. His lips were cool, his skin still chilled from the outdoors. It was over before she could think about enjoying it, and then she was out the door and standing beside him in what looked like a garden. Paved walks, flower or vegetable beds separated by stone and neatly trimmed shrubs sprawled along the east side of the house.

"Where are we?"

"We just left the old servants' entrance," he explained. "Around the corner is the kitchen and the herb garden, but we're going to walk over that hill to one of the dairies."

The three dogs raced around the corner of the house and greeted them with eager, wagging tails. Kate petted each one, which seemed to satisfy them. "How many cows do you have?"

"I couldn't say. I have over a dozen farms, leased, of course, in this part of Leicestershire. Come along." He took her hand. "I'll show you how we make Stilton cheese."

Kate hated to sound ignorant, but she had to know. "What exactly is Stilton cheese?"

"The most famous cheese in England," he declared. "It's only made in the shires of Leicester, Derby and Nottingham. It's a wonderful ending to a meal, with fruit especially. Do you like blue cheese or Roquefort cheese?"

"I like blue-cheese salad dressing."

"Ah," he said, sounding pleased. "Then there's hope."

The next hours sped by as Kate followed William and the excited dogs over the countryside and eventually back to the stables, where the dogs were left behind. She climbed into a battered old truck, and William drove her to the buildings where the cheese was made. He proudly explained the complicated process, starting

with the formation of curds from the pasteurized milk
and ending with the large rounds of cheese being tested
for ripeness and texture by a skilled cheese grader. The
white-coated workers were too polite to stare, but Kate
saw the curious looks that were cast her way. Will in-
troduced her to several people as his "American cousin"
and behaved as if there was nothing unusual in escort-
ing someone through the refrigerated rooms stacked
with cylinders of cheese.

"Where do you sell them when they're done?"

"We have distributors for markets, both in Britain
and overseas."

"I could buy one in Rhode Island?"

"I would imagine. Maybe not one of mine, but I can't
imagine that it would be hard to find Stilton anywhere."

They shared a lunch packed by Mrs. Goodfellow:
small thermoses of chicken soup, crusty bread and fruit
salad. William made tea in his small office, then drove
her through several small towns, past Rutland Water,
a huge reservoir, and past countless acres of pasture-
land.

"Hawthorn," Will explained, pointing to the hedges
that bordered much of the land. "May Blossom, we call
it."

"This is beautiful country. I'm glad I was able to see
this part of England." She looked at her watch. It was
after three and past time to find a train back to London. "Do you have a train schedule somewhere? I
should get back to London before dark."

"Are you certain?"

"I think it's probably a good idea." Kate didn't look
over at him. Instead, she watched the stone house ap-

pear in the distance. Of course, she'd like to stay, but she was tired of knowing he was with her because of his loyalty to his grandmother. Everything he'd done for her, he'd done because his grandmother had insisted or begged or coerced, which included taking her along to Thorne Hall and entertaining her today. Naturally she'd like to believe it was because he found her irresistible, but Kate knew better.

William didn't answer. He drove the truck into the stable and parked it beside the Jaguar. He turned off the engine and ignored the dogs who had followed them inside and whined for attention. He looked serious as he turned to her and spread his arm over the back of the seat. His fingers grazed her shoulder. "Is there some reason in particular you want to leave so soon?"

Kate faced him reluctantly. He was the kind of man she'd dreamed of loving: strong and kind, sexy and quiet; nice to old ladies and pesky dogs. He looked good with a little mud on his left cheek and a faded old jacket that had one of the pockets half ripped off. She liked him better today than she had that evening at San Lorenzo's. She liked the man who had kissed her in the dim hall and had found boots for her to wear. She was more than a little bit in love with him, and it was her wedding day. Her ex-wedding day.

"No answer?" He gave her a half smile. "Or no reason?"

"No idea what to say."

"Then say you'll stay. At least until tomorrow. I'm sure Mrs. Goodfellow has planned to serve tea now, and she's probably been working all day on something special for supper. You'll hurt her feelings if you leave."

"I don't believe Mrs. Goodfellow cares one way or the other."

He leaned closer to her. His fingers brushed the shoulder of her jacket and touched the ends of her hair. "Oh, that's where you're wrong, Katie Stewart." His voice was soft. "She and Harry are chattering now, wondering who you are and why I brought you here. Beth has recognized the brooch, you see. Naturally she's curious as to why you wear it."

His wonderful lips moved closer. If she wanted to, which she did, she could put her hands on either side of his face and pull him to her. "Your grandmother told me not to take it off. I think she's afraid I'll lose it."

"She has her reasons." He tilted his head closer. "We both do."

Kate forgot to take the bulky gloves off before she touched his face. He held her against him as they kissed, and Kate wrapped her arms around his neck to draw him close. It was as if she'd been waiting all day for him to hold her again. She parted her lips slightly, at the gentle insistence of his tongue, and soon his mouth slanted over hers in a kiss that burned through her body until she no longer remembered her frozen toes. She forgot she had toes. William tossed his gloves aside, unzipped her coat and slid his bare hands along her waist. Kate turned, to kiss him better. Their tongues tangled, and her heart expanded in her chest until she thought she could no longer breathe.

He slid his warm palms under her sweater and cupped her breasts. A gasp of startled pleasure escaped her as his roughened skin moved above her bra and unfastened the center hook. She realized she'd been waiting for him to touch her, waiting for this breathless, aching feeling that swept across her skin. She managed to take off her gloves, then slid her fingers along the soft skin at the back of his neck and wound them through the thick waves of dark hair. She couldn't help pulling him closer, couldn't help wanting his hands on her breasts and his thumbs teasing her nipples to hard peaks. She couldn't help wanting him, couldn't help wishing they were anywhere but sprawled on the seat of an old truck in a dark garage that smelled faintly of horses and old leather.

She wished they were in a bed.

"Come on, boys! We'll go—" Mr. Goodfellow's booming voice reverberated through the large stable, along with the dogs' excited barks.

Kate pulled away from William's arms and hoped her brain would kick in and restore her to the sensible woman she knew she was. Or she used to be, she thought, gazing with regret at William's lips.

"Sorry, lad!" Harry called as he backed out of the building. "I didn't know anyone was in here. I thought you forgot to close the door."

"You're a dangerous woman, Kate," William said. He hooked her bra with experienced fingers, tugged her sweater over her hips and swept a lock of hair from her flushed cheek and tucked it behind her ear.

"That's a compliment, isn't it?" She liked the idea of being dangerous.

"Yes. I suppose."

"You're not exactly white bread yourself, you know." She discreetly adjusted her sweater. Her bra felt two sizes too small.

"It's not always easy to be around you," he muttered, reaching for the handle on the door. "I forget where I am."

"You do?"

Will got out of the truck and shut the door. "Yes, I do. In lifts, taxicabs, trucks." He shook his head in mock disgust as he walked around to Kate's side of the truck and opened the door. "I'll have to listen to Harry's apologies for the rest of the weekend. Now you have to stay. Otherwise, he'll think he scared you off."

Kate chuckled. "I can't."

"Can't or won't?"

"Shouldn't."

"I'll have Mrs. Goodfellow move you to the east wing, if you like." He lowered his voice to a whisper. "And there are locks on all the doors. You're not required or expected to sleep with your host."

Oh, she was definitely in love with him, Kate decided. Which was exactly why she shouldn't stay. She was lonely and vulnerable and on the rebound. And tonight should have been her wedding night. Her first night as Jeff's wife, and now she felt nothing but relief at the thought of escaping that particular fate. "Unlike other guests of past dukes?"

"Most likely," he agreed. "I'm sure they all had mistresses. House parties at Thorne Hall were probably excuses for illicit sex with someone else's willing wife." He took her hand. "Come on. Let's see if Beth baked scones for us. I'll tell her you're staying the night."

"I guess I could," Kate conceded. Being in love with William Landry didn't mean she had to run out the front door like a frightened virgin. Because she wasn't, either frightened or virginal. She was twenty-five and free to enjoy the company of a handsome man. She wasn't the first woman to fall in love with the Duke of Thornecrest and she wouldn't be the last. He'd kissed her as if he'd thought she was the most desirable woman in the world. He'd taken care of her when she was sick and had smiled at her jokes. He didn't seem to mind when she teased him, either. He was kind and thoughtful and very, very sexy.

And as dangerous as a runaway train.

"YOU SHOULD BE in the morning room or the library," Mrs. Goodfellow muttered. "I would've fixed you a proper tea, using the old duchess's porcelain."

William stretched his legs beside the worn oak table. "That's ridiculous and you know it. I always have my tea in the kitchen, with you."

"You have company." She sniffed. "I could've done it up right, with the silver and all." Mrs. Goodfellow shot Kate an apologetic look. "You would've liked something a little fancier, I know you would, though you're too polite to say so."

"I like your kitchen," Kate assured her. William wanted to laugh at her expression. Kate didn't want to hurt the housekeeper's feelings, but he could tell she meant her words. She looked more relaxed in the midst of the oak-beamed kitchen than she had drinking tea at Browns. "It's very comfortable," she added after helping herself to another scone.

Mrs. Goodfellow wiped her hands on a red-checked cloth. "You're feeling better, I hope?"

"Yes."

"Neither one of you must have had much sleep last night. I'm planning a late dinner, so there's time for a nap."

He watched in fascination as Kate's cheeks turned pink. Obviously the fact that he'd cared for her still embarrassed her. She and his plump housekeeper discussed the unpredictability of the stomach flu, then moved on to a discussion of the evening's dinner menu. Mrs. Goodfellow launched into the virtues of cooking with a gas stove, and Kate appeared to be enthralled. William poured himself another cup of tea and lathered another scone with clotted cream. He never took company in the kitchen. He entertained rarely, usually only during the fox-hunting season. He didn't hunt himself, but some of his friends waited each year for nearby Melton Mowbray's famous hunts. He hadn't known it would be so enjoyable to sit in a warm kitchen and listen to the women chatter.

The women now moved on to Mrs. Goodfellow's favorite subject: her grandchildren. Her daughter lived in nearby Oatley, she explained, and the three children, two boys and a girl, visited Thorne Hall often. Kate thought that was wonderful. Her mother had died only a few years ago, she confided to the housekeeper, shortly after her father's death. Mrs. Goodfellow clucked sympathetically. Kate told her of her three older sisters, adding that as the youngest she'd always been considered the black sheep of the family. She'd never known her grandmother, but she'd been very close to her great-aunt, she told the older woman. In fact, Kate continued, her aunt had given her this brooch. Mrs. Goodfellow admired it and gave William a curious look.

"Yes, it's real," he said, answering her unspoken question. He wiped his mouth with a napkin and tossed it on the table.

"But that means—"

"It's been in Kate's family for years," he interrupted, unwilling to discuss the legend behind the brooch. He could see the pleased sparkle in Mrs. Goodfellow's eyes from across the room. Kate hid a yawn, which gave him the perfect opportunity to excuse them both from the kitchen. "Go take a nap," he told her. "I have several hours of paperwork waiting in my study." He looked at the clock over the hood of the massive black stove. "It's almost five-thirty. Come down at seven-thirty, and we'll have a drink before dinner, all right?"

"It sounds perfect." She took her empty mug and plate to the sink, then hid another yawn and smiled. "Sorry. I guess it's all this fresh country air."

He wanted to kiss her, but he settled for holding open the kitchen door and watching to make certain she turned left at the end of the hall.

"She's a lovely girl," the housekeeper said from behind him.

Will turned around and leaned against the wall. "Yes," he agreed. "She is."

The housekeeper nodded toward the black sweater hanging on the back of Kate's empty chair. "I never thought I'd see the day."

"The brooch, you mean?"

"That, and your bringing a young lady to sit in the kitchen like the mistress of the Hall. None of those city airs about her, y'know."

"Kate's here for the weekend. Nothing more." Somehow the thought wasn't pleasant. William

frowned and crossed his arms in front of his chest.
"Pitty wanted her to see the portrait in the dining
room."

"And what do *you* want?"

"Peace and quiet," he declared. "I want that damn
brooch out of my life once and for all."

"And what about that nice young lady? She looks at
you as if you hung the moon."

"The stars, too," Harry added, entering the kitchen
through a side door. "You've a smitten look yourself,
lad. Best be careful, or you'll find yourself tied to a noisy
female till your dyin' day." He dodged the red dish towel
his wife attempted to swat him with and gave her a swift
hug.

"I'll be careful," William promised. He picked up
Kate's sweater and threw it over one arm before leaving the room. "I'll be *very* careful," he repeated to himself as he went down the hall. He would keep his hands
off her for the rest of the weekend, he promised himself. He would not kiss her. He would not make love to
her hour after hour in the dark, quiet hours of the night.

He could, however, deliver her sweater and her
troublesome pin to her. He would smile and be polite
and then he would turn away, go into his study and
concentrate on cheese.

IF ANYONE ASKED what she had done in England, she'd
have to say she'd drunk a lot of tea, Kate mused, tug-
ging her turtleneck over her head. She'd tell her sisters
about the tea; she wouldn't tell them about the Englishman or this visit to a stranger's country estate or
about having the stomach flu. She kicked off her shoes
and her socks, hung her jeans in the closet, and turned

down the lace coverlet. None of this "resting on the bed" stuff. She was going to treat herself to a real nap between crisp cotton sheets, with the thick covers pulled up to her ears and the shades drawn shut against the fading afternoon light.

Yes, her trip to England would be highly censored, much of it her own little secret. Memories she would not share. She was about to climb into bed when a knock came at her door.

"Yes?"

"May I come in?" William asked.

"No. I mean, not yet." She looked about for something to put around her. She couldn't answer the door wearing nothing but panties and a bra, even though he was slightly familiar with the bra. She hurried into the bathroom and grabbed one of the large yellow bath towels to wrap around her. Then she twisted the doorknob and opened the door a few inches. "Sorry," she said, peeking out, "I, um, was just—"

"I didn't mean to intrude," he said, avoiding her eyes. "You left your sweater in the kitchen. I didn't want you to think you'd misplaced the brooch."

He held out the sweater to her, and Kate opened the door wider in order to take it. She smiled. "I'm sorry. I feel a little silly hiding behind a door but I was just about to get into ..." She stopped, feeling even more ridiculous.

"Bed," he finished for her, and let go of the sweater as if it were on fire.

She could see half his face, half of his rueful smile. "Yes," she said. She heard him sigh.

"Close the door," he said. "Now."

She kept it open, about eight inches from its frame, and asked, "Why?"

"Because I'm a weak man," he explained. "I look at your shoulders and your soft skin above that towel and I remember the way you felt under my hands a while ago. I'm remembering the taste of your mouth and the scent of your hair and how your fingers touched the back of my neck when you reached up to kiss me."

Kate's knees weakened.

"Shut the bloody door, Katie," he ordered.

"All right," she whispered. She put her hand on the door and gave it a push. It closed with a miserable finality. But William was right, she reminded herself. They couldn't, shouldn't make love to each other. She wasn't the kind of person who had one-night affairs, who slept casually with anyone who attracted her. She leaned against the door and waited to hear his footsteps move down the hall. He had lots of women. Scores of them, probably. She remembered how Jessica and her friends had stared at her from their exclusive corner table at San Lorenzo's. She was only one in a long line of the duke's conquests.

"I apologize," he said from the other side of the door. "I was out of line."

"No. I've been kissing you right back," she admitted. *And I've fallen in love with you, too. How about that for a laugh?* What was she afraid of? Getting hurt? She'd already been dumped once, by one of the most boring men in New England. He'd said they didn't have anything in common, that she wasn't exciting enough. Now a duke was apologizing to her for wanting to make love to her, for finding her desirable. "Thank you," she said.

"What on earth for?"

"For wanting to," she told him. "I know you must have lots of women—"

He swore, turned the knob and pushed the door open. "What on earth gave you that idea?"

She gripped her towel, making certain it was securely fastened. She wished her arms weren't so pale. "Well, don't you?"

William glared down at her. "I've never brought anyone here, alone, until now. You are absolutely driving me insane, too. What the hell are you thanking me for, anyway?"

"Y-you look at me as if I'm beautiful," she stammered. "I appreciate it."

He stared at her as if she'd surprised him. "You are beautiful," he replied. "Why wouldn't I look at you? Of course, there are times when I wish you were a little less stubborn and a little more willing to follow directions—"

"Like, 'Shut the damn door'?" Kate grinned. "Very fierce, very duke-ish."

He shut the bedroom door and turned back to her. "I don't think 'duke-ish' is a word."

"It fits you."

He bent his head and kissed her lightly. "You should have kept the door closed," he said when he lifted his lips from hers.

She reached for him, standing on tiptoe to put her hands around his neck. "It's more fun talking to you in person."

"But I'm not going to talk anymore," he said, lifting her into his arms. He carried her over to the bed and set her gently on the mattress.

"Even better," Kate murmured, looking into his dark eyes. There was nothing to fear, except making a fool of herself. He would never have to know that a foolish American tourist had lost her heart to a very eligible duke. He would never realize she wanted to believe in fairy-tale endings.

She could hide how she felt, she promised herself. He bent down and kissed the pulse in the hollow of her neck, and she shivered at the sensation.

He stopped, lifting his head to look deep into her eyes. "Are you cold?"

"No. I'm not cold." She reached for him, smoothing her hands over his wide shoulders. He would never have to know she'd fallen in love.

9

WILL DRAGGED HIS LIPS lower, to the tempting cleavage above the towel, and unfolded the towel to reveal the woman underneath. She was beautiful, in scraps of lace and nothing else. Will unhooked her bra and slid it from her shoulders. He felt as if he was unwrapping a special package, a gift he had been waiting to open for a very long time.

"You are very beautiful," he said, hoping to convince her.

His lips found hers, seeking her warmth with his tongue. She responded to him with a longing of her own, and her hands wound around his neck to hold him against her. When he finally released her, it was only to remove his clothes and toss them onto the rug. Kate turned on her side and watched him, entranced by his hard male body. His shoulders were more powerful than she'd imagined, his legs muscular and long. He didn't seem to mind that she looked at him. He was comfortable with the way he looked, of course. He was used to being admired and treated like royalty.

Dark hair covered his chest and tapered to an intriguing path down his abdomen. His arousal was obvious, yet he seemed not to notice her surprise at the size of him. She wanted to reach out and touch him, wanted to feel that odd combination of steel and satin under her fingertips, but Kate stopped herself. Her experience was limited; he might not like it.

"You're beautiful, too," she said, then couldn't believe she'd spoken aloud. The dim light from the window shades gave the room a cozy, shadowed feeling, where everything seemed muted and unreal. She felt disoriented and yet she didn't want William to leave. She wanted him with her, wanted to feel his skin against hers. She wondered what he would feel like inside her, what it would be like to make love with him.

Kate started to bring the sheet over her shoulder, but he stopped her. One large hand reached out and grasped the sheet. "Don't cover yourself," he said, his voice gruff. "You needn't be shy with me."

"It's hard not to be," she admitted. "You keep looking at me."

He sighed. "Of course I do, Kate. I want to look at you and touch you and make love to you all at the same time. I've wanted you since the first time I saw you," he said, surprising himself by admitting the truth.

"You wanted the brooch."

"No," he said, approaching the bed. "The brooch would have been a favor to my grandmother. I wanted you." He traced a finger along her cheek to her lips and brushed them with tantalizing softness. "I didn't understand it myself."

"Neither do I."

"Do we have to understand it?" He slid into the bed beside her, brushing skin like warm satin.

Kate shook her head.

"I'm going to make love to you now." Will leaned over her, and his mouth touched hers with exquisite softness. Ever so slowly he deepened the kiss as Kate parted her lips to allow him entry. They kissed for long moments. His hands moved to her breasts and cupped their weight in his palms. His thumbs teased her nipples, sending pangs of desire through her. He kissed the corner of her mouth and her throat. His lips sought the column of her neck, the hollow near her shoulder. Kate felt herself melting, as if every inch of muscle and bone was dissolving under his touch.

She was still on her side, her breasts brushing his furred chest and her nipples sensitive and aching from the friction. He seemed to know what she needed, and he bent down and began to caress one breast, then another, with his lips. Finally, after long minutes when Kate thought she would melt into the mattress, he took one peaked bud into his mouth. The exquisite pressure was almost her undoing. Shafts of pleasure lunged downward as his lips tugged and teased. His free hand smoothed her hip and lowered her panties.

She moaned and moved closer to him, and felt his hard arousal touch her thigh. He lifted his head and pushed her gently onto her back, smoothing his hand over her abdomen as he kissed her mouth. His hand moved lower, and he dragged the lace past her ankles and tossed it aside. He urged her thighs apart and touched her where she was warm and wet. His tongue moved deep into her mouth as he slipped one finger inside her. Kate trembled with the pleasure he gave her as his hand moved over her and his palm cupped her flesh.

He was taking his time, she realized, but she wanted him inside her. She didn't want to wait any longer to know how he would feel sunk deep within her. He withdrew his finger and stroked her flesh, centering the spiraling heat in one throbbing place.

"Do you like my touching you?" he whispered. She looked into his eyes, eyes dark with passion.

"Yes," she managed to say, and gasped as he slid two fingers into her. She closed her eyes and let the sensations sweep over her as he moved his hand for long moments before gently withdrawing his fingers.

He nudged her legs wider apart and slipped a condom over his hard length before entering her. He took her slowly, to prolong her pleasure at his entrance. She gripped his hips and arched against him, and Will knew he was lost.

She was liquid and slick and panting, and Will forced himself to slow his thrusts. He wanted to pound into her, needed to bury himself over and over again in her tight, welcoming warmth. He stopped, buried fully within her. She stilled, and his mouth found hers. He moved his tongue deep into her mouth, stifling her soft whimpers. Her hands smoothed the sides of his face and tried to draw him closer, even though it was impossible.

Sweet Kate, he thought, the fine thread of control snapping as his arousal swelled even larger. He withdrew slightly, then moved his hips forward, gliding and withdrawing for long, breathtaking minutes until he felt Kate tighten around him. He lost all sense of time and space. He forgot who he was. All he knew was Kate, her sweet breath and her satin skin and the sleek, tight warmth that surrounded him. She pulled him closer, so when shudders shook her body he still had possession of her mouth and heard her passionate whimper as she climaxed. A few more thrusts and he joined her, burying himself into her over and over again as spasms shook him.

KATE FLOATED back to reality very slowly. He had moved from her, but his arms were around her and her face was buried in his chest. She felt sated and spent. She felt as if she'd just learned what lovemaking really was. She hadn't felt awkward or shy. She'd only known him for a week, but he was achingly familiar, as if she'd known him all her life. As if they'd been making love all their lives. She inhaled, trying to memorize his scent, and the hair on his chest tickled her nose.

"What are you doing?" His voice was sleepy.

"Trying not to sneeze." She wasn't going to tell him that she was trying to remember the way he smelled of lime and leather and English rain.

William lifted his head and looked down at her, his expression amused. "Sneezing's allowed, Katie."

"I thought you were asleep."

"No. Yes. Almost." He turned on his side to face her. "Do you want me to leave?"

"No." She nuzzled his chest, and he reached past her to pull the covers over her bare shoulders. "Sleep here."

Will hesitated. "All right. For a while."

"You don't have to," she said, lifting her chin to look up at him.

"I'll make love to you again," he warned. "I don't want to hurt you."

"You won't hurt me."

He ran a large hand along her waist and smoothed her hip. "You're so soft. And so small. And I want to make love to you all over again." He nuzzled her neck and tucked her firmly into his shoulder.

Kate closed her eyes and murmured an agreement as the warmth of his body wrapped around her and lulled her into sleep.

SHE DREAMED of butterfly kisses on her knees, of gentle fingertips moving across her thighs and higher, releasing heat and causing a heavy, familiar throbbing between her legs. She dreamed a gentle pressure spread her legs apart, and she heard a voice whisper, "Wake up."

She didn't want to. She didn't want the dream to end, didn't want to wake up alone and cold in the hotel bed. She wanted to pretend that William's warm breath fanned her thigh, that his lips sought to release the aching pressure building inside her, that his tongue slipped—but it wasn't a dream, she realized, slowly coming awake. She was naked and aroused, and William was touching her with his fingers and his lips and his tongue. She arched, whimpering with bliss and awe, but he splayed one hand across her abdomen to hold her still while he pleasured her. Kate yielded as the familiar throbbing echoed through her body. He held her against his mouth and brought her to exquisite release, and only then did he move above her.

William entered her swiftly, and she arched to meet him as he filled her with long, smooth strokes. He made love to her as if he couldn't get enough of her, as if he needed to prolong the time together as much as was humanly possible. He held himself hard against her and groaned as he climaxed. His lips found her throat, and he traced the rapid pulse until his own heartbeat eased and he knew he wasn't going to die from sheer pleasure.

"Not a dream," she murmured.

"No." He lifted his head so he could look into her eyes. They were a deep forest green now, and sleepy. "No. Just a man who couldn't wait any longer for you to waken."

"I'm glad," she said, closing her eyes. He lifted himself from her, and she turned on her side toward him but she didn't open her eyes. He fixed the covers and propped his head on his hand to study her. Her cheeks were flushed, her lips slightly swollen and pink. Her hair lay wavy and tangled against the white pillowcase. He should be embarrassed for taking her twice. He should be appalled that he'd made love to her while she slept, but he hadn't been able to resist tasting her.

And if he didn't get out of this bed, he'd be more than willing to do so again, he realized. She would awaken thinking the Duke of Thornecrest was a lust-crazed animal. He didn't know what had come over him, but a hot shower and a couple of hours of bookkeeping should help. He slid out of bed and picked up his clothes. Next to his boots, so close he was lucky he hadn't stepped on it, lay the brooch. William resisted the urge to kick it under the bed. Still pinned to the sweater, the brooch shone with an ominous glitter.

KATE AWOKE in the dark and realized she was alone. She moved her hand across the mattress and felt the cool sheets. He'd been gone awhile. She knew she should get up and take a shower and dress for dinner, although how she was supposed to sit across from the table from him after his mouth had... Well, Kate decided, she didn't regret the experience. He'd made her feel sexy and desirable and beautiful. He'd looked down at her as if he'd loved touching her, loved being inside her.

She just wished she was more experienced at country weekends and sex-filled afternoons. Was she supposed to stroll downstairs as if nothing had happened? Well, Kate decided, she'd have to try. She didn't really have any other choice.

"KATE?" William knocked on the door when she was brushing her hair. Kate looked at her watch and realized it was seven-thirty already. She'd soaked in the tub for a long time, wondering how jilted and jobless Kate Stewart from Rhode Island had managed to be in an English mansion surrounded by luxury and having great sex with a duke. Kate put her brush on the makeup table and reluctantly went to the door.

"I'm ready," she called. Bracing herself, she opened the door. She pasted a casual smile on her face and lifted her gaze to his face. He swallowed hard, then smiled a small, tight smile that showed he was a bit ill at ease, too, and Kate realized everything was going to be all right.

Will lifted a bottle of wine. "Have a drink with me in the study."

"That would be nice." She stepped out of her room and turned left. He caught her arm.

"No, I meant my personal study," he said, turning right. "Follow me."

"Okay," she agreed, intrigued. She hadn't seen this part of the house before. He led her down the wide corridor, past several closed doors, until he reached the wide double doors at the end of the hall. He twisted the knob and pushed the door open to reveal a wide living room lined with tall windows, dark green drapes and cherry bookcases. A massive desk sat at an angle in the corner, a leather chair behind it. A fire burned in the fireplace in the center of the wall that faced them, and a small round table was set for dinner in front of it.

"I told Mrs. Goodfellow we'd eat here. I thought it would be less formal. Do you mind?"

"Of course not." She thought it was very romantic.

Will led her over to a forest green sofa, its faded velvet surface covered with needlepoint pillows. "Mrs. Goodfellow gives me a pillow every year for Christmas," he explained. "Toss them aside and make yourself comfortable." Wineglasses on a tray perched on the marble table, along with a selection of cheeses and crackers on a gold-edged plate. Mrs. Goodfellow had outdone herself.

"This is a nice surprise." She sank into the couch and tucked her legs underneath her. The room was warm, the fire crackling and snapping, and she was glad he'd chosen to show her his study. "This must be the room you really live in. It's like your own apartment within the house."

"Yes." He uncorked the wine and filled the two glasses with golden liquid. "I thought you might like it. And the salon downstairs is a little overwhelming for two people."

"You must have wonderful parties, though."

He handed her a glass and joined her on the couch. "No. Not really. I save my social life for London."

She gave him an odd look, as if she didn't believe him. He knew she hadn't been convinced when he'd told her she was the first woman he'd brought here alone. She probably thought he did this every weekend. "It's true," he insisted. "I don't bring women here."

"Never?"

"A house party or two during hunting season, perhaps." William wanted her to know she was special, but he was afraid to let her know she was special. "Up until now this was—is—a private place. I've had guests, of course, but I don't sleep with them here. I've kept those parts of my life separate, you see." He didn't stop to question why today was different, why Kate was the only woman he'd ever wanted at the Hall. He touched her glass with his. "Until now."

Kate took a sip of the wine. "You've gone to a lot of trouble for a diamond pin."

"I don't make love in order to buy jewelry." His gaze dropped to her sweater, a brown turtleneck that blended with her hair. "You're not wearing it tonight."

"I forgot."

"Good."

"But it's my good-luck charm. My aunt promised it would bring my heart's desire," she said, taking another sip of the wine.

"And has it?"

"I'm in England. That's a start."

"If your heart's desire is a great deal of money, then I would say you have more than a start."

She changed the subject. "Your grandmother told me to wear it all the time."

He frowned. "My grandmother has odd ideas."

"It's not odd to want to regain something that once belonged to you. I just don't think that it was stolen. So it's not really out of the family. Didn't she ask you to find some old books or diaries?"

He refilled their glasses and moved the cheese tray within reach. "She did. She's attempting to discover if one of my ancestors actually went to America with the brooch."

"Then she believes me, at least a little." Kate helped herself to a cracker and a piece of cheese. "I'd like to know that myself. Have you found anything?"

"No. Not yet." He smiled. "I suppose you'd like to help me locate them."

Kate forgot the food in her hand. She'd love to see more of the house, especially if she had a chance to find something as wonderful as old diaries. "Are they in the library, or do we get to go up in the attic?"

"The attic, I think. I've already searched the library."

She leaned forward, her eyes shining. "When?"

"Tomorrow."

"Why wait? We have time tonight," she argued. "It's still early."

He should have known that an English attic would fascinate her, although exploring dusty boxes of books wasn't exactly what he had in mind for tonight. But he couldn't refuse her something so simple when she looked so eager. "All right, if that's what you want."

"I do."

He leaned forward and kissed her. Her lips were pliant and sweet and tasted of chardonnay. "Are we pretending this afternoon didn't happen?"

"I don't think I could," she admitted with her usual frankness. She put her glass on the table and turned to face him. "Is that what you want, to pretend it didn't happen?"

"No." His voice was rough as desire surged through him again. He wanted to make love to her on the couch right now, wanted to feel her tight around him and hear her little gasps of pleasure. "No," he repeated, clearing his throat. "I couldn't pretend and I couldn't forget." He touched her cheek. "I don't want to."

"Neither do I."

He kissed her again, telling himself that he could stop whenever he wanted. After all, he still had some control left. Not much, but enough to keep his hands off her before dinner. "Don't leave tomorrow," he whispered against her mouth. "Stay one more day, and I'll take you back to town Monday or Tuesday or whenever you like."

She twined her arms around his neck. "I have a flight home on Tuesday."

"Monday, then." She was leaving already? The thought bothered him. He hadn't stopped to consider that he would not see her again and he would want to.

"All right. That will give us time to find the books."

The heaviness in his chest eased. "I don't give a damn about the books." He kissed the little spot beneath her ear and felt her shiver, then attempted to regain control of himself before he made an idiot of himself. "I'd better ring for dinner before we start taking our clothes off."

"I think you're right." Kate released him and gave him an embarrassed smile. "I'm afraid I have that reaction when you kiss me."

Her honesty overwhelmed him. That's what he liked best about her, William decided. Or one of the things he liked best. "I'll be more careful in public places," he teased. He would have to be careful in every way, he decided, crossing the room to the call panel. He was in danger, serious danger, of falling in love with her.

And that was the last thing he intended to do. He was a bachelor, a happy bachelor. Or, he amended, a *contented* bachelor. Marriage might start out with soul-shattering sex and sweet words and promises of love, but there would be no happily-ever-after if you were the Duke of Thornecrest.

"HAVING FUN?" he drawled.

Kate took her head out of a large trunk and sneezed. "Excuse me." He handed her a handkerchief, and she sneezed again.

"We've found no boxes of books," he informed her. "Isn't it time to give up?"

"No." She'd never had so much fun in her life. She'd left the search for books to William after discovering the trunks in a corner of the enormous attic. They were stuffed with antique clothing of all colors and sizes. Pastel dresses of silk and muslin, with lace trims and velvet edging and pearl beads, were packed carefully in layers. Kate held a pink gown in front of her and pictured waltzing around a ballroom. "Your ancestors were very well dressed. Somebody went to a lot of trouble to preserve these clothes."

"A Landry throws nothing out. I believe that's why we can barely move up here."

She put the pink gown aside and unfolded an ivory one. A wide band of lace dipped low across the bodice, and the long, puffed sleeves were trimmed to match. "I think duchesses were quite thin."

"Take it downstairs and try it on," he said. "If you like, I'll have Harry put the trunk in your room. Better yet," he added, eying the low neckline of the dress, "I'll have the trunks put in my room."

"Every girl loves to play dress-up, you know."

"I'm beginning to realize that." He shoved his hands in his pockets while she dove into the trunk, anxious to see if there were shoes to match.

"You should have daughters," she said. "They'd love it up here."

"We breed only boys. That and bad husbands."

"That's why these clothes are still up here." She lifted out stacks of underwear, or what she guessed was underwear. She'd have to figure out what went where later. "Little girls would have found them ages ago."

"I suppose. Have you reached the bottom yet?"

"Almost." Her fingers touched something hard, but she was afraid she'd topple into the trunk if she tried to get her hands around it. "Come here, Will, and help me. There's a box or something."

"After this we're leaving," he said, coming over to stand next to her. "I'll tell Pitty I couldn't find a thing."

"Right down here, on the side. Can you feel anything?"

"Got it." He hauled up a packet of leather-bound books tied with velvet cord. "Must have belonged to one of the duchesses."

Kate reached for the books. "Let's see."

"Downstairs," he said, looking down at her with a hungry expression. "You can read later. After you put on that white dress and after I remove it."

Kate's heart flipped over in her chest. "You are such a romantic man."

William looked appalled. "You don't know me very well."

"Maybe not," she said, wishing she could say what was in her heart. She wished she could tell him that she'd fallen in love with him. She wished she could tell him what this week had meant to her. Instead, Kate turned away and scooped up the dress and a pile of undergarments and hugged them to her chest. "Come on, then," she said, keeping her voice light. "Let's hope the duchess was a size 9."

"WAIT," she said. He heard the rustle of silk. "Okay, now open your eyes. You can't see all of me until after you button me up."

Will opened his eyes and touched the creamy fabric that hugged her skin. He held his breath and hooked the tiny buttons along Kate's spine. She'd piled her hair on top of her head, and when he remembered to breathe, he planted a tiny kiss on the nape of her neck and held her waist between his hands. "Will you turn around now?" he asked.

"It fits," she said, and swirled to face him. "I can't believe it fits."

"It's quite beautiful," he agreed. He didn't point out that the duchess who had worn the dress must have been at least six inches taller and not as well endowed as Kate. Creamy skin swelled above the lace in a dress meant to tantalize. "The dress is quite old, early to mid-1800s, I'd guess. Those are the dates written inside the books."

"What kind of books are they?" He watched, fascinated, as Kate attempted to tug her bodice higher, but the fabric didn't budge.

His hands tightened at her waist. "The packet contained four novels and two diaries. Pitty will be beside herself with joy. I'm going to kiss you now."

He bent closer, and she tilted her head back. "Be careful."

He stopped. "Why?"

"The dress," she murmured a scant inch from his lips. "It's very old."

"I'm not concerned with the dress." He pulled her closer and heard the oddly erotic rustle of silk as he held her against him and took her mouth. She was soft and pliant, and William thought he could kiss her for hours and never tire of touching her. He moved lower, touching his lips to the tops of her breasts. Lace tickled his chin, and he felt Kate's trembling hands tangle in his hair. He kept hold of her waist and backed her against the paneled wall. Then he braced both arms on the wall and looked down. Her lips glistened, and she looked up at him with her heart in her eyes.

Damn. He should have known a woman like Kate would fall in love. He should have realized that she wouldn't have given herself to him so freely unless her heart had been involved. He should be upset, but all he could think was to make love to her again, as soon as possible. "Lift your skirts," he said.

"Why, sir!" Her eyes twinkled. "Whatever do you have in mind?"

"Lift your skirts and I'll show you," he whispered, kissing the corner of her mouth. "You like that dress so much you may as well keep it on."

"The undergarments are, um, open down there." She grabbed hold of the fabric at her hips and lifted it. "Do you think this is the reason?"

"I don't care." He unzipped his fly and readied himself, then helped Kate with her petticoats. He found the opening in the silk underclothes and paused to make her ready for him before taking her. "Open your legs," he commanded softly. He felt her legs tremble. "And put your arms around my neck."

She did, and he slid inside her, then cupped her buttocks in his palms and pulled her tight against him. Kate moaned.

Will stopped. "Am I hurting you?"

"No," she said. "You feel so good—"

He stopped her words with another thrust and made love to her with slow strokes until she tightened around him and cried out. As he moved still deeper, sensation overwhelmed him, making him forget everything but Kate around him, Kate's breath on his throat and her pliant body under his hands. He felt himself shatter inside her, and knew he wanted only this, only Kate, forever.

"WHO'S ALICIA?"

"I haven't the foggiest idea," he drawled, looking at her. "Now that you're naked and in my bed, I think I've lost the capacity to think."

Kate blushed and pulled the sheets up higher. She'd taken most of the pillows and propped them behind her so she could study the diaries. "Her name is written in the inside covers of the diaries. I don't think she was a duchess. She talks about making her 'come out' and meeting suitable young men. Her father is mentioned often, and her governess, too." Kate looked down at William. He had one pillow tucked behind his head and he turned to face her. There was a gleam in his eye she was beginning to recognize. "I've only looked at a few pages, but doesn't she sound like a young woman to you?"

"Yes. A debutante, if she's talking about her 'come out.'"

"How can we find out who she was?"

He sighed. "We can read the diaries. Tomorrow."

"I meant besides that." She glanced over at the chair beside the bed where the gown lay in a tangle of silk and lace. "Don't you have family records?"

"Oh, most definitely. Kilos of them." His hand slid under the white sheet and caressed her thigh. "Turn off the lamp."

"I think I like these country weekends," Kate sighed, setting the book on the table. She turned off the bedside light and waited for a few seconds for her eyes to adjust to the darkness.

"Come here."

"This was much more fun than getting married."

His hand stopped its tantalizing journey up her thigh. "What are you talking about?"

"I was supposed to get married today, remember?" Kate rearranged the pillows and lay down on her side to face Will.

"He was a fool, but considering the circumstances, I'm glad you're in England instead."

She kissed his chest. "You're absolutely right. I'm quite content with the way things have turned out today. After all, I wore an ivory dress and have been made love to three times."

"Four," William murmured, reaching for her in the darkness.

10

"THE YOUNG LADY is still sleeping?"

"I assume so." Kate was asleep, all right. Snuggled in the middle of his bed with the covers pulled up to her chin and her dark hair spread over the pillows, she'd looked content, as if she were sleeping in her own bed. Now *that* was a frightening thought. And a strangely appealing one.

Will had no desire for Mrs. Goodfellow to discover where his house guest had spent the night. She was as enthusiastic a matchmaker as his grandmother. He selected a mug from the cupboard and poured himself a cup of coffee. His housekeeper stood at the stove frying strips of bacon. The smell made his mouth water, and his empty stomach growled.

"Should I bring up a tray for her when breakfast is ready?"

"No," he said quickly, too quickly. Mrs. Goodfellow's eyebrows rose as she stared at him. "I'm sure Kate would like to sleep late."

"I see." She turned her attention back to her cooking and poked the bacon with a spatula. "Your grandmother called this morning. I told her you weren't awake, and she seemed quite put out."

"She'll survive." Will took his coffee to the kitchen table. He sat down, and Harry shoved part of the Sunday newspaper over to him.

"She told me three times to tell you to ring her as soon as you woke. She wanted to know if you'd found any other journals, she said. And she *also* wanted to know if Miss Stewart was still here. How many eggs do you want?"

"Three. No, four. Did you tell her?"

"Yes," Mrs. Goodfellow answered. "I said she was here and nothing more. It's none of my business, either, I told her."

Harry eyed William over the edge of his newspaper. "Hungry this morning, are you?"

William frowned and didn't answer.

"It's pouring today. You're lucky you did your tourin' yesterday," the older man continued. "The little miss wouldn't like getting wet."

"She probably wouldn't mind," Will said. "A little rain wouldn't bother Katie."

"Mebbee you're right." Harry nodded. "She's the first one you've brought home, and I'm mighty glad to see she doesn't walk around with her nose up in the air."

Mrs. Goodfellow placed a plate piled high with fried eggs and bacon in front of Will, then returned with silverware and napkins for both men. "She's a lovely young lady. You could do worse."

"I don't intend to 'do' at all," Will declared. "I'm taking her back to London tomorrow, and then she returns to the States."

Beth handed her husband a plate identical to Will's. "Why don't you go with her, then? Have a little vacation and then bring her back here? It's time there were children—"

"Children? I'm not cut out for fatherhood," Will drawled, though suddenly the vision of little girls playing dress-up in the attic pleased him. He shook his head as if to clear it. Landry men had sons. One and only one son. There would be no giggling daughters and no teasing older brothers. There would be no children because there would be no marriage. "Or wedded bliss, either," he added. "Despite what you or Pitty wish to believe, I am not interested in marriage, no matter how many women visit the Hall."

Mrs. Goodfellow brought her coffee to the table and sat down. "Nonsense! She's the first one you've brought home all by herself. And you'd make a lovely husband, you would, even if you are impatient and bossy."

"I have lots of patience," he argued, thinking of the days spent touring London with Kate. "More than you know."

The housekeeper sniffed. "Oh, there's lots I know," she said, unimpressed. "I know you're nothing like your father or your grandfather. Silly men, with a taste for women who didn't suit them at all. Not like you. Now, finish your eggs so you can take Kate's breakfast to her. I made some apricot scones I think she'll like."

William looked around hungrily. "Where are they?"

"You can have one each," she told the men. "The rest are for the young lady."

William started to protest, but Harry caught his eye and winked. "You may as well give up, lad. If she says the scones are for Miss Katie, then that's where they'll go."

"Miss Katie isn't the duke around here," he grumbled, picking up the last piece of bacon on his plate.

"And you're not smart enough to make her a duchess, either," Mrs. Goodfellow retorted. "I wash my hands of you, I really do."

Kate a duchess? She'd looked like a queen in that
ivory dress. William pushed his plate aside and finished his coffee in one swallow. "I'm going for a walk,"
he said. "The fresh air might clear my head."

"You do that," Mrs. Goodfellow said. "But I don't
expect that the cure for what ails you lies in the east
pasture."

Will ignored her and left the kitchen, grabbed his
oldest coat and hat from the hall and slipped out the
back door. The dogs wagged their tails and jumped
around him, begging for attention, so Will petted them
before he set out for a long, wet walk. He would let Kate
sleep, he decided. Alone. And he would spend some
time away from her and try like hell not to hurry back
to the house to wake her and watch her smile.

KATE KEPT her eyes closed. She lay snuggled under the
warm blankets, afraid that if she opened her eyes she
might discover that yesterday had been a dream. Making love with Will and falling asleep in his arms were
definitely the stuff of an overactive imagination, or the
result of eating chocolate-chip ice cream before bed. If
she opened her eyes, Kate reasoned, she would see the
bathroom door of her plain St. Giles hotel room.

She didn't want to see the bathroom door of her hotel room. She wanted to see an ivory gown sprawled
across a spindly-legged chair and the rich velvet drapes
hiding the morning sun, but most of all she wanted to
open her eyes and look into William Landry's familiar
and handsome face.

"Kate? Are you awake?"

An intriguing male voice, she thought, and one she
recognized. Kate risked opening her eyes slowly, hop-

ing she was really in the master bedroom at Thorne Hall. Will came closer to the bed. He held a large silver tray, and Kate smelled coffee. "Hi," she whispered. "I'm awake. I think."

"Maybe this will help." He set the tray on a delicate round-topped table and poured coffee into a porcelain cup. Kate struggled to sit up, keeping the blankets covering her naked body, and Will waited for her to prop two pillows behind her before handing her the cup of coffee.

"Thanks," she said. "Is it very late?"

"After eleven."

Kate grimaced and took a sip of the coffee. "It isn't like me to sleep so late." She glanced at his amused expression. "*None* of this is like me, but I guess you wouldn't believe that."

He walked over to the window, shoved his hands in his pockets and stared out the window. "You don't have any idea what I believe, so drink your coffee and get dressed. The rain has stopped for now, but it doesn't look as if it's going to stay clear for long. We could take a walk through the gardens or drive over to Hallaton. It's the sort of picturesque English village you would enjoy, I think."

It wasn't fair that he looked so darn handsome in the morning. He wore dark slacks and a soft blue cotton shirt and he looked as if he'd slept for twelve hours. "Can we do both?"

"Of course. The day is yours." He turned to face her, but he didn't come closer. She'd foolishly hoped he'd kiss her good-morning, so she hid her disappointment by drinking the coffee as quickly as possible and burned the inside of her mouth.

"Mrs. Goodfellow baked scones for you," Will said, turning away from the window. "There are some here on the tray, and more in the kitchen."

"They look delicious! Give me twenty minutes to finish this coffee and get dressed," she said.

"There's no rush." He looked nervous, as if he regretted last night and wanted her out of his bed and his room as quickly as possible.

Kate tucked the sheet higher above her breasts. "May I borrow a robe?"

"Certainly." Will perched on the side of the bed and looked down at her. "I'll fetch you one of mine."

"Thanks." She smiled, and to her relief he smiled back at her.

"I've been wondering about your plans," he began, reaching out to tuck a strand of her hair behind her ear. "Must you leave tomorrow, Kate?"

"I really think I'd better get back to London."

"That's not what I meant, Kate. Do you have to leave England right away?"

Kate set her empty cup on the nightstand before answering. "Yep. I have to find a new job."

"You could live a long time from the sale of the brooch." He stood up, crossed the room and disappeared through a door.

"I can't do that. If there was some kind of family emergency, I would sell it in a minute, but I can't just get rid of an heirloom because I don't want to start job hunting." She wished he understood. "It wouldn't be right. Besides, I like the brooch. Somehow I feel that it's brought me luck." There was no "somehow" about it. She'd met William because of the brooch. She'd experienced a trip to England that she would never have believed possible.

"You could stay in England for a while longer," he suggested, as he came across the room with a navy silk robe slung across his arm. "There is so much you haven't seen."

"I'll save my money and come back," she said, keeping her voice light.

"Can you postpone leaving for a few more days?" He sat down on the bed and handed her the robe.

"I can't change the tickets without a big penalty."

"I'd be happy to take care of that," he offered. "If you'll allow me."

"I can't. That wouldn't be right, either."

He sighed. "I thought that would be your answer, but I had to try. Are you certain you won't stay? Just for a few more days, of course. We could drive north, to Scotland. There are plenty of gift shops there, too. In castles, no less."

He was teasing her again, Kate realized. He'd lost his solemn expression and was once again the lighthearted man from yesterday. She would have given every souvenir in her hotel room to stay, to journey on to Scotland, to stay here at the Hall, to wake in the morning and talk with William about the plans for the day.

"It's time I got on with my life," she said, trying to convince herself. "I'll start by sneaking back to my room."

"You don't have to sneak at all. There's no one else around."

"I keep thinking your grandmother will appear and scare us both to death."

"She called this morning, actually." He reached over to the table and refilled her coffee cup. "She wants to know if we've found anything."

"We don't know if we did or not." Kate couldn't believe she'd forgotten about the books. "That's what we should do today."

William grimaced. "Later," he declared. "Much later." He looked down at her and sighed. "Have I kissed you good-morning yet?"

"No." Her heart lightened. "I was wondering if you'd forgotten."

"No." He set her cup back on the silver tray and leaned closer. "That's all I've thought about since I woke up." His lips brushed hers in a sweet reminder of last night's passion before he slowly lifted his mouth from hers. "There," he whispered. "I feel better."

"Me, too." She reached for his shoulders, and the sheet dropped. William's gaze lowered to her breasts. "Why don't you come back to bed?"

He kissed her neck. "That is an excellent idea. I think I will."

Kate unbuttoned his shirt and smoothed her palms across his bare chest.

He stood to remove his pants, then climbed into bed beside her. "Come here," he said, pulling her close.

She was beginning to be familiar with his body, to know what touches made him shiver and what kind of caresses made him moan. He pulled her on top of him and wound his arms around her back while he kissed her, but she wriggled from his arms and dragged her lips across his chest and lower, to his abdomen and the rigid flesh below. She took him in her hand and into her mouth while he gasped with pleasure and surprise. After long moments he pulled her above him and, tumbling her onto her back, took her with swift strokes.

Kate wanted it hard and fast. She wanted to remember everything about making love to him: his touch on her breasts, the feel of him filling her, the taste of him on her lips.

Kate lay in bed long after Will rose and retrieved his clothes.

"Are you certain you have to leave tomorrow?" He grinned at her and poured another cup of coffee.

"Yes. I'm sure." Kate avoided his eyes and took the coffee. She didn't want him to see the truth. She didn't want him to realize that a silly tourist had fallen in love with a charming duke and dreamed of happily-ever-after in a cheese factory.

IF ANYONE HAD TOLD HIM that he would spend a perfect weekend with a woman he barely knew, William knew he would have smiled. If anyone had warned him that he would fall in love with her and want to keep her with him always, he would have been quite overcome with mirth. And if anyone had told him that he would feel sharp pains in the vicinity of his heart as he drove this particular woman through the gates of Thorne Hall and out of his life, he would have wiped the tears of laughter from his eyes and choked back a rude reply of disbelief.

William's hands tightened on the steering wheel as he guided the car down the winding driveway. He didn't feel at all like laughing. He didn't want Kate to leave and he didn't know how to persuade her to stay. He dared a glance toward her, but her face was turned to the side window.

"We should be in London by three o'clock," he said, trying to erase the memory of making love to Kate this morning. They'd stayed in bed long after they should have risen. They'd made love one more time in the murky morning light while a light rain drizzled against the windows. There hadn't seemed to be any reason to hurry out of bed.

Kate turned away from the window and looked at William. "That's fine. What about Pitty?"

"I'll tell her you won't sell the brooch," he said. He wished he'd never laid eyes on the thing. Even now it sparkled on the lapel of Kate's coat, reminding him of how he'd met her. Was Pitty right? Was the legend of the Thorne Diamond true after all? He'd fallen in love with the woman wearing it. He'd acted like a lovesick fool for days. What on earth was the matter with him? An early midlife crisis or a simple case of infatuation?

He didn't know. And wasn't about to find out.

"I can tell her myself," Kate offered, "if you don't mind stopping at your house first. Besides, I think I owe her that much."

"All right, if you like." He drove in silence for a few minutes longer, negotiated the turn onto the main road and headed toward the highway. His heart felt heavier by the minute. "Pitty won't accept your decision easily, you know. She wants the brooch back in the family."

"I know. I wish we could have found something in the diaries that would prove my ancestors didn't steal it."

"We didn't exactly have time to read diaries." They'd spent their time in other, more interesting ways. They'd made love, taken walks yesterday and had visited with Paula and Sam when they'd dropped in to say hello.

Sam had winked at him, and Paula had taken him aside and whispered how pleased she was that he had finally found someone special. He'd agreed with her; he hadn't told her of Kate's plans to leave.

Then they'd eaten an enormous dinner of pheasant and wild rice, walked in the gardens in the rain and, after warming each other in his wide bed, made love again.

William took a deep breath and attempted to keep his thoughts focused on the conversation. "Besides, Pitty will spend weeks poring over every word. You've challenged her, you see. She must prove there was no Landry in America after all."

"Will you let me know what she finds?"

"Yes."

"No matter what?"

"Of course," he promised. "I'll tell her about the clothes, too. They should probably be in a museum." He would package the ivory one and send it to Kate as a souvenir. She'd looked beautiful in the gown. She'd looked beautiful without the gown.

"Save one or two for some little girls to discover someday." She smiled a bit ruefully. "That's what attics are for."

"I'll remember that," he promised. "Unless you'd prefer to stay in England and remind me?" He pictured little auburn-haired girls parading around the Hall in lace flounces and satin slippers, and dark-haired boys running with the dogs, and laughter and chaos echoing through the once-quiet rooms of a home that once was too big for one lonely man. He reached for her hand and held it within his own. "There is no reason why you can't stay . . . a while longer."

"So Pitty can convince me to sell my pin?"

"So I can convince you to stay in England."

She didn't answer immediately. Finally she spoke into the silence. "For how long, William?"

He shrugged. There was no way he could answer that question. He could promise nothing, after all. This weekend, this past week had been wonderful, but intimate relationships had a way of disintegrating. It was just a matter of time. "Until you want to return home, I suppose. Nine days in England is not a long time. You've lots more to see."

"As much as I'd like to stay, I think it's time I got back to the real world," she said. "This has been wonderful, of course. Thorne House and Thorne Hall and Stilton cheese and priceless jewels and a duchess serving tea have all been very exciting. Especially when I didn't expect to experience any of it. But it's time for a dose of reality."

"That sounds quite ominous."

She smiled. "I didn't mean it to be."

"I'm not certain I can let you go," he said, staring at the road. Kate looked at him. He could feel her gaze on his face. "It doesn't seem at all right," he muttered, mostly to himself.

Kate didn't reply.

William took his hand from Kate's and turned the car onto the highway and headed south, to London. She was the kind of woman who wanted promises of love and lots of children. She'd told him she'd dreamed of making apple pies and pot roast. Kate would settle for nothing less, he knew. And she was right to do so.

He was the wrong man for her.

SOMETHING INTERESTING had happened in Leicestershire. Pitty could tell by the proprietary way William removed Katherine's coat and handed it to Mary. His hands had lingered on the American's shoulders in a most loving way. It wasn't her imagination, either, Pitty decided. She nodded when Mary asked if she wanted tea and settled herself in the wing chair. She wondered if the young people would sit on the sofa together.

They did, to her great delight, although they were quite discreet about sitting apart. Mrs. Goodfellow had revealed nothing, but Pitty could read between the lines. You didn't reach the age of eighty-nine without learning a few tricks. She smoothed her chartreuse skirt as if she had all the time in the world. "Did you enjoy the country, Katherine?"

"Very much."

"Kate had a touch of the flu," William interjected. "But she's feeling much better now."

"Good." She turned back to Kate. "And the painting? Did you see the brooch?"

"Yes, but—"

Pitty held up her hand to silence the girl. She wasn't in the mood for unhappy news right now. She'd rather wait for a bit, she thought. At least until she'd watched the lovesick expression on her grandson's face a little longer. "Tell me what you found," she ordered, noting the packet of books William had dropped on the table.

"Diaries," he said. "We haven't figured out whose diaries, precisely, but from what we've read we assume it is a young girl about to make her debut into society in 1812."

He'd said "we" three times. How encouraging. The brooch had worked its magic after all. Pitty resisted the urge to clap her hands and order champagne. "And there were no names?"

"She used initials to indicate the people in her life. I didn't read every page, of course."

"Neither did I," Katherine admitted. "We found several trunks in the attic. One of them was filled with beautiful gowns, and the diaries were at the bottom."

"Clothing, too? How very fascinating!"

William leaned forward. "You've never gone through the attic, Pitty?"

She shook her head. "I only lived in Leicestershire for a few years. Long enough to give birth to your father and realize what an idiot your grandfather was. I moved to London after your father entered school. And after your parents died, I hadn't the time or energy to begin rummaging through the family attic."

"You should see the gowns," Katherine said. "They're beautiful."

"I made arrangements with Mrs. Goodfellow to hang them and air them out. We can decide what to do with them after you've had a look," William explained.

"Good." Mary brought the tea tray into the living room and set it on the table. "We'll have some tea and discuss what to do about the brooch," she declared. "Thank you, Mary."

"There really isn't anything to discuss, Pitty. Kate isn't going to sell it."

Pitty ignored him and looked at the young woman instead. "Are you quite sure, my dear? The Thorne Diamond has been missing for a very long time, and I would be willing to pay a great deal to have it back."

Kate's voice was soft. "I don't want to sell it."

"If you ever change your mind, you have only to contact either William or me, of course."

"I will."

Pitty smiled. "Let's have our tea now, shall we? William, will you pour or shall I?"

"I THINK SHE TOOK IT quite well, don't you?" Kate whispered after Pitty left the living room.

William frowned, wondering what the old girl was up to now. She'd excused herself after she'd finished her tea, said her goodbyes to Kate and had taken the books with her when she'd left the room. "Perhaps," he said. "I didn't think she'd give up so easily."

"Easily?" Kate chuckled. "She's been trying for more than a week to buy the pin. Maybe she finally accepted the fact that she can't have it."

"You don't know her. She's the most stubborn and persistent person I've ever known."

"I'm sorry, Will. I hope this doesn't make things difficult for you."

He looked at her, obviously surprised. "I never wanted the damn thing, Kate."

"You didn't?"

"Well," he amended, "only at first. To placate Pitty so I could return to the Hall. She had her heart set on it, and I hate to refuse her, you know. She's all I have." He reached for Kate, and she went willingly into his arms. "Stay, Katie. Stay with me."

Kate waited for him to say the words, to say something about love and forever, but they never came. "We've been over this before."

He took a deep breath. "Cancel your flight home and live with me at the Hall. We'll travel." He kissed her.

"We'll walk the dogs and make love and explore the attic. You haven't seen Paris or Switzerland, either, and Florence is perfect in the spring."

"You make it hard to say no."

"Then don't. Say yes and we'll pick up the rest of your things at the hotel and return to Leicestershire in the morning."

"You're asking me to live with you," she stated. She was definitely in love with him, with a power and depth she'd never experienced before, but how did she fit into his life? "Why?"

The question stymied him. He frowned. "Why?" he echoed.

"Why do you want to live together? Great sex? Companionship? You want someone to eat scones with in bed?"

"Yes. I don't know," he said quietly. "I only know I don't want you to leave."

"I could only stay *if* I was very much in love with you, and maybe not even then."

"We've only had a week."

He'd smoothly ignored the "I" word, she noted. Kate smiled, but it wasn't easy. "It was one hell of a week."

Will touched her face with gentle fingers. "Don't say no yet, Katie. Give me a chance to change your mind. I'll take you to the airport tomorrow. When does your plane leave?"

"Maybe that's not such a great idea." She'd cry all over his fancy car and embarrass herself.

He ignored her comment. "When does your plane leave?"

"Three-ten. I should be there around one-thirty, though."

"I'll pick you up at twelve forty-five. We'll have lunch together at the airport after you check in." He smiled. "*If* you check in."

She would not fall into his arms, she told herself. She would not blubber about how much she loved him and how much she wanted to stay in England. She would not tell him she wanted marriage and his babies and a fiftieth wedding anniversary party with their children and grandchildren. She took a deep breath and hoped she wouldn't make a fool of herself. "And what if I stayed, Will? What if I fell in love with you? What then?"

"I don't know, Katie. I've never been in love before and I'm not sure I want to be."

"At least you're honest."

He grimaced. "Not always, but I'm trying to improve." He stood up and took her hand to lift her to her feet. "Come on. I'll take you back to the hotel."

"Thank you." She couldn't believe her vacation would end tomorrow. Tomorrow night she would be on a bus heading to Rhode Island, and Anne would meet her at the bus station and take her home. But home to what?

"I'll ring you later," he promised, sliding the coat onto her shoulders. "I'm not going to give up."

"Falling in love isn't so terrible, you know." Kate turned in his arms and lifted her face for his kiss. Mary scurried out of the room and left them alone.

His lips brushed hers. "It's the very worst thing that could happen," he whispered.

"WHAT IN BLOODY HELL have you done?"

"Don't swear at me, Willie." Pitty patted his cheek as she passed by him and plopped onto the sofa. "I did it for your own good."

William made an effort to control his temper. A Ming vase hitting the wall would make a most satisfying sound. He took a deep breath and willed himself to stay calm. "How could stealing the Thorne Diamond be for my own good? Except, of course, if you were caught and locked up. *That* might be in my own best interest."

"Don't be sarcastic. Have you asked the American to marry you?"

"Of course not. Where is it?"

"That's what I thought." She sighed and patted the couch cushion beside her until he reluctantly sat down. "Have you told her you love her?"

"Where is it, Pitty?" His grandmother eyed him silently, waiting. Was it that simple, he wondered? Was falling in love as easy as admitting he didn't want to live another day if Kate wasn't part of his life? "No," he admitted. "I haven't."

"Idiot," she murmured, and patted his face affectionately. "You still don't believe in the diamond's power, do you?"

"Tell me where it is and I'll return it to Kate with your apologies. I can tell her it fell off her coat and we found it in the closet."

"Or maybe you believe after all," she mused. "You're in love with her, of course. Any fool can see that. Are you going to ignore your chance for happiness?"

"I will call the police. I will tell them you have become a kleptomaniac in your senior years and I will have you shipped to a sanatorium in Wales. You can spend the rest of your days looking at the sea and counting gulls."

"I would have preferred an Englishwoman, naturally. So I've decided to give this one more chance. The brooch has gone to Jessica's flat. With a note from me requesting she wear it to the theater tonight, as part of an experiment. You'll accompany her, of course."

"Why would I do that?"

"I think you'd like to know if you're in love with Katherine because she's, well, *Katherine*, or if the brooch is responsible."

"The damn brooch has nothing to do with loving Kate," he snapped.

"Then prove it," she demanded.

"You could toss the cursed thing in the Thames for all I care, but it belongs to Kate and she will be heartbroken when she discovers it's missing." He rose from the couch. "I'm going to Jessica's to get it back."

"She's not there. She's meeting you at the Palace." Pitty looked at her watch, then back up to Willie. "You have fifteen minutes, but I suppose you are fine in those slacks."

"You planned this right down to the minute, didn't you?"

Pitty shrugged but she couldn't hide her satisfied smile. "You're making a grave mistake by letting Katherine slip out of your life, but perhaps she wasn't meant to be a duchess after all. Try the pin on Jessica and see what happens."

"My grandmother's insane," he muttered under his breath as he left the room. "Absolutely insane." Now he had to put on a clean shirt and head to the West End. He would meet Jessica, find some excuse for taking the brooch and hurry to the St. Giles to return it before Kate realized it was missing. Damn Pitty and her bloody legends.

11

ANNE CALLED at seven-thirty. "I keep hearing about bomb threats at Heathrow," she said. "Is it safe for you to leave?"

"That happened a few days ago. It's been quiet since then," Kate assured her.

"Call me if you get delayed. Have you had a good time?"

How should she answer? Would the phrase "good time" describe falling in love with a duke? Kate chose her words carefully. "Yes," she answered slowly, "I had a good time." Then Kate explained she'd met a wonderful, handsome, kind Englishman who had showed her around London.

"Bring him back with you," Anne demanded. Her voice was loud and clear through the telephone receiver. "I want to meet him. So will the others."

"I'll ask him," Kate promised. "I don't know what to do, Annie. I've fallen in love with him."

"It's not a rebound thing from Jeff?"

"No. I thought it could be at first, and then I realized it wasn't the same feeling at all." She didn't add that he was a duke. Annie would never believe her. "He's a very special person. Very kind."

"I still can't believe you met someone."

"Well, I did." She also left out the part about spending the weekend at his house in the country. Her older sister would have a fit. "I think Aunt Belle's pin brought my heart's desire after all."

Anne chuckled. "You have quite an imagination, Katie."

"Not always." She decided to save the news about the brooch's worth. She wanted to see her sister's face when she told her that the oversize pin was worth a fortune.

"Are you seeing him tonight?"

"He's going to call. He's taking me to the airport tomorrow. He says it's his last chance to talk me out of leaving."

Anne sighed. "That's so romantic." Then her voice sharpened. "Be careful, Katie. You've only known him a week."

"I knew Jeff for five years, and look what happened."

"You have a point," Anne conceded. "But you can't be too careful these days."

"Don't worry," Kate assured her. "He is the nicest, kindest, most honest man I've ever known."

WILLIAM DIDN'T PAY attention to the play. He endured the first act and attempted to make his excuses during intermission, but Jessica met some friends. He bought a drink while Jessica disappeared into the ladies' room with Lady Taylor and Penny Southington for most of the intermission. He had no choice but to return to his seat and wait for her. She slipped in beside him as the theater grew dark, and then it was too late to leave. He couldn't very well unpin the brooch from above her right breast and run out of the theater in the middle of *Les Misérables*.

The brooch twinkled at him, as if mocking his predicament, but it didn't have the same glow as when Kate wore it. Maybe her coloring had complemented the stone better. He was a fool. He knew it. He could have been with Kate; instead, he was sitting in a darkened theater peering at his watch and wondering how many songs were left before the French Revolution ended. It had to be the longest musical in London.

At least he'd proved one thing: the ugly brooch had nothing to do with loving Kate. He shifted restlessly in the narrow seat and glanced at Jessica's chest to make sure the brooch was still there. He would return it, even though now it was so late he would have to wait until morning. Kate would be frantic if she discovered it was missing. Hopefully she hadn't noticed, and he could return it to her with no harm done, except the embarrassment of explaining Pitty's role in its disappearance. Then all he had to do was convince her to remain in London, with him—forever.

But would Kate stay? Not without a promise. Not without a few encouraging words of love. Well, maybe he could manage that. He loved being with her, loved making love to her, loved the way she laughed after she teased him. He loved her perfume and her hair and her eyes and her very luscious body. He wanted her to live with him, wanted to wake up with her in the morning and climb in bed beside her at night. Did all that add up to being in love? Was it enough to last a lifetime?

KATE FELL ASLEEP with the light on and the television repeating the evening's news. She'd packed and repacked, trying to find room for the souvenirs she'd bought. She even folded the paper bags from the gift shops and tucked them inside the suitcases, too. She couldn't bear to leave anything behind. The weekend caught up with her eventually, and she fell exhausted onto the bed and woke up at seven o'clock the next morning.

Would he ask her to stay again? She wanted to say yes, but what would happen after that? He wanted an affair; she wanted a marriage. She was in love with him and couldn't picture loving anyone else. The past nine days had been the most wonderful days in her life. Leaving England would be the most difficult thing she'd ever done, and yet she didn't know how she could stay.

Kate knew she had to make a decision before twelve-thirty. She could return to Rhode Island and settle into a new job and a new apartment. She could remember her time in England as a sweet interlude or she could take a chance and stay here with William, for however long.

The sun was shining, so she left her coat hanging on the back of the hotel door and, too edgy to pace inside her small hotel room any longer, headed outside into the bright morning air. She walked down Charing Cross Road, past the now familiar bookstores, toward Trafalgar Square. Unwilling to face bangers and bagels at the hotel, Kate bought a newspaper from the man on the corner of Leicester Square and stopped at one of the French *pâtisseries* that dotted the West End.

She ordered coffee and a giant jelly doughnut and sat down in the corner. Pretending she did this every morning, Kate drank her coffee and read the article on Heathrow and the terrorists; the situation didn't sound too serious. She skipped through the political scandals and paused at photos of royalty. Princess Diana had hosted a reception for the American Red Cross yesterday afternoon. Prince Charles had given a speech across town. Lady Helen Taylor, cousin of the queen, had attended the theater as part of a friend's birthday celebration. Lady Helen was a pretty blonde, Kate noted, but the tall woman standing beside her looked familiar. Kate looked closer. She was William's friend from San Lorenzo's. And she wore the Thorne Diamond brooch pinned to the bodice of her dress.

THERE HAD TO BE A MISTAKE. It couldn't be the same brooch—her brooch. Kate hurried back to her hotel room, grabbed her coat from its hook and looked down at the bare lapel. Then she realized she could have left it pinned to her black sweater. She'd packed quickly, after all. She might have missed it; she'd been so intent on finding space for the coffee cups, teapot and various boxes of bath gels. Kate tossed the contents of her suitcase onto the bed and pawed through the clothing, then crawled on the floor and searched under the bed.

When had she last seen it? Kate sat on the floor and tried to remember. She'd worn it on her coat in the car. Her hair had caught on one of the prongs, and she'd untangled it when she took off her coat at Thorne House.

Thorne House. There had been no call from the Duke of Thornecrest last night. There had been no word from him this morning. He'd offered to buy the brooch; yesterday she had refused to sell it, once and for all. Had he been pretending to accept the fact that it would not be returned to his family? Had he been pretending all along, about everything?

She blinked back tears. Crying would do no good. Finding the brooch was the answer. Kate searched the small room. She stripped the bed, checked between the mattress and the wall and found nothing. She had to face the facts. The brooch was gone, transferred to the bosom of another woman, a woman Will had dated before he'd met her. He hadn't called last night, though he could have come over when she was asleep. If he'd knocked on the door and received no answer, he could have decided against waking her. But why hadn't he called this morning?

Because he was guilty? Because he'd finally obtained what he wanted all along? Kate didn't want to believe the man she loved would do such a thing, but she hadn't wanted to believe Jeff was calling off the wedding and marrying someone else, either. She'd thought he was joking.

There was nothing funny about losing something worth a quarter of a million pounds. There was nothing funny about believing she was loved, only to discover it was all a lie. She'd been foolish to insist on wearing the pin instead of storing it in a vault. She'd thought she was safe with Will Landry, too.

Kate slung her purse over her shoulder and grabbed the newspaper, folded so the photograph of the pin was displayed. She wanted an explanation, and she wanted it in person.

"I'M SORRY, miss, but His Grace is not at home at the moment." Mary wiped her hands on her apron and looked distressed. "I'm afraid I can't invite you in."

"Lady Thornecrest isn't home, either?"

"At the moment she's not receiving visitors."

Of course she wasn't. Why risk being confronted with the accusations of a furious American tourist? "Tell the duke that Katherine Stewart was here and will be going to the police about her missing jewelry." She gave the little maid the paper. "Tell him the Thorne Diamond's on page thirty-one."

"I will, miss." The maid nodded politely and took the paper. "Will there be anything else?"

Kate hesitated, her anger and pain threatening to bubble over. Screaming on the duke's doorstep would accomplish nothing. She couldn't believe they were going to ignore her, but naturally that was exactly what they would do. Who would the police believe, a middle-class tourist on a budget tour or a respected member of British society? Pitty would back up anything Will said, of course, so it would be Kate's word against theirs.

She was having trouble believing it herself, but what else could she think? The pin was gone and entrance to Thorne House denied. Her love affair with William might never have existed, their days spent together a figment of a lonely woman's imagination. Kate blinked back tears and turned away from the elegant entrance of Thorne House.

She wished she'd never come to England.

"GONE? What do you mean, *gone?*" William leaned forward, unwilling to believe what he'd just been told. His fingers tightened around the paper wrapping of the roses he'd stopped to purchase on Oxford Street.

The young woman behind the counter shot him an affronted look and rifled through the pages on the counter until she found the one she wanted. "Miss Stewart has checked out, sir."

"Katherine Stewart? Are you certain?"

"Yes."

"How long ago?"

The woman frowned, obviously annoyed by his persistent questions. She looked back down at the paper before replying. "Sometime before noon."

Before noon? Will remembered to thank the young woman before stepping away from the reception counter. What on earth was going on? It was only twelve-thirty, and Kate had left without him. He returned to his car and picked up the phone. Maybe she had left a message with Pitty.

A few minutes later Will slammed down the phone and hurriedly put the Jag in gear. Pitty had babbled tearfully about a newspaper clipping and a visit from Kate and other things that didn't make sense. All he knew was that Kate was at the airport, preparing to leave him, and he had to stop her before it was too late.

"KATE!"

She heard the voice as she stood in the middle of the Body Shop, trying to to decide whether or not to buy a wooden comb. She didn't need a wooden comb, but she was trying hard to think of ways to keep busy, to keep from thinking of William and the way he'd betrayed her. She'd already bought a crossword puzzle, four packets of English chocolate and a bottle of unblended Scotch from the duty-free shop.

She must attract weird men, she thought, ignoring the voice calling her name. The voice couldn't possibly belong to William. He wouldn't come to find her, to tell her he loved her, to return her brooch and apologize. Things like that *definitely* did not happen to her.

"Kate!"

She felt a hand touch her shoulder, an achingly familiar touch. She drew a quick breath and turned around. He had the gall to smile. She stared up at him.

"You stole my brooch," she said, wishing she could punch him in the stomach, but her hands were full of packages.

"No, I didn't."

"I want it back."

He looked uncomfortable. "I didn't steal it, Katie."

"Then you've brought it to me."

William looked down at her free hand. "Are you going to buy that comb? I'd like to get out of here and talk to you."

Kate dropped the comb back in the bin and held out her hand, palm up. "Give it back to me. I want to go home now."

"The brooch is still at Thorne House, with Pitty. She wants to talk to you."

"I'm through talking to either one of you," Kate declared. "I'm getting on a plane in an hour and when I get home I'm going to get a lawyer and find out how to get Aunt Belle's pin back. I know I don't have a snowball's chance in hell here, when you're practically a member of the royal family."

"That's not true," he protested. He took her hand and pulled her out of the store. "The brooch is safe and waiting for you. Come home with me. I'll return it to you."

Kate shook her head. "I don't believe you. You and your grandmother stole the brooch. You just had to have it, didn't you? Were you going to send me a check or were you just going to steal it outright?"

He gripped her hand tighter and led her past the ticket counters toward the exit. "We didn't steal it," he insisted. "At least, I didn't. Pitty was to have explained and apologized this morning, but she's a little under the weather right now." He slowed down as police scurried to bar the wall of exit doors. "What on earth is going on?"

"Another bomb threat," a British Airways employee beside them explained. "They're closing down everything until they determine whether or not it's safe to use runway two."

"For how long?" Kate asked. Her sisters would be frantic when they heard the news.

The man shrugged. "It's difficult to say, miss. It could be hours before we're cleared. No one can leave the airport and no one can enter until further notice."

William took her elbow and steered her away from the alarming scene. "Let's have some tea. There's something I want to—"

"I need to call Anne. She's the one picking me up tonight."

"Go ahead," he said, indicating a nearby wall of public telephones. "I'll wait here."

She noticed he didn't argue about her leaving. What had happened to the loving man who had asked her to stay in England and travel with him? Kate looked at her watch as she hurried across the wide corridor. Anne wouldn't be home, but she could leave a message on her sister's answering machine to let her know that there was nothing to worry about.

Kate glanced back at the tall man whose protective gaze was still on her. Oh, there was something to worry about, all right. The thieving duke still owned her heart.

"YOUR FLIGHT today is canceled," William declared, trying not to smile. He had conferred with the ticket agent after the announcement that the airport had been reopened. "You're not going anywhere tonight."

"You don't have to look so happy about it," she grumbled.

He tried to hide his satisfaction with the news. Five hours in this airport had crawled by like eight. Kate hadn't had much to say and neither had he. Which was fine. He didn't want to say what he had to say in the middle of Heathrow during an IRA bomb threat. "They'll start flying again in the morning and your flight will most likely be one of the first ones to depart. They suggest you return by six-thirty." He didn't add that he had other plans where her departure was concerned.

"Well—" Kate eyed the row of plastic seats beside her "—I suppose that won't be too bad."

"You're not staying here for the next twelve hours," he said. "And neither am I. You're coming home with me. Now."

"No." She sounded tired, and her eyes were suspiciously bright.

"Don't be an idiot. You can stay at Thorne House until morning. You will sleep in a comfortable bed." He stood up and picked up the bag by her feet. "Don't fight me, Katie. It's the least I can do after...everything that has happened."

"Will you give me the brooch?"

"Yes. Of course." He was doomed to spend the rest of his life regretting he'd ever set eyes on the damn thing. "After you've listened to what I have to say."

THORNE HOUSE was different. A faint odor of fresh paint still clung to the air, but the sheets had been removed from the furniture and the paintings were in their proper places. Kate longed to explore the downstairs rooms once again, but resisted asking Will for another tour of his home. She couldn't let herself be distracted from what she needed to do: get the brooch and leave for home. She could cry when she got on the plane. She was looking forward to it, in fact. But for now she wouldn't let Will see how much he'd hurt her. She had no intention of spending the night, either. She would pick up her pin and leave, no matter how many times the Duke of Thornecrest protested.

They took the elevator to the upper story, and Mary greeted them when they stepped into the foyer.

"How is Pitty feeling?" he asked the housekeeper.

"She's in the living room. I've prepared a simple dinner. You can eat whenever you're ready."

William thanked her and ushered Kate into the living room. Pitty, wearing somber knit slacks and a black sweater, waited for them in the wing chair. "My dears," she said, wiping her eyes with a lace-edged handkerchief. "I have been so worried about you."

"As you can see, we're fine. And you? Are you feeling a bit livelier now?" He sat on the couch with a grateful sigh and pulled Kate down to sit beside him. She attempted to pull her hand from his, but he held on tightly and pretended he didn't notice her efforts to distance herself.

"I'm better," Pitty sighed. "Much better."

Kate looked at the elderly woman's pale skin and couldn't help worrying about her. "Have you been sick?"

"Yes," she nodded, clutching her handkerchief. "A touch of that flu that seems to be plaguing the neighborhood, I suppose, but now that you're here . . ." Her voice trailed off as she looked at her grandson. "I'm still in trouble, aren't I?"

He nodded. "Kate would like an explanation."

"And my pin," Kate added.

Pitty nodded. "Of course. I must confess, I stole your brooch yesterday. Or rather, I instructed Mary to remove it from your coat."

"But why?"

"The legend," Pitty replied, looking toward William. "Explain it to her, dear."

William rested his arm on the back of the couch and, still holding her hand, turned to face Kate. "You're going to think we're all mad, I'm afraid." He smiled down at her. "But be patient, just for a few more minutes. My grandmother believes that the brooch—*your* brooch— brings happiness in the form of marital bliss to its owners. She is firmly convinced that the reason there have been unhappy Thornecrest marriages in the past four generations is because the brooch disappeared."

"Aunt Laurabelle said it would bring my heart's desire," Kate murmured. "I wonder if she knew there was something special about the pin. I can't believe she knew it was valuable, though. She kept it in her dresser drawer, with her other jewelry."

Pitty nodded. "It has always been passed down from mother to daughter, but unfortunately there have been no daughters in many, many years. I'd give a great deal to discover how it ended up with your aunt." She paused. "Do happy marriages run in your family, Katherine?"

Kate thought for a moment. "Why, yes, I guess they do."

Pitty gave William a triumphant look. "That proves it, you see. I was right all along."

He didn't look as if he wanted to agree. "Give Kate the brooch."

The old woman rose, went to the sideboard and picked up a small enamel box. She crossed the room and handed it to Kate. "Take it, my dear, and wear it with happiness."

Kate opened the box and saw the pin nestled securely inside. "Thank you."

William frowned at his grandmother. "Why on earth are you wearing black?"

"I'm in mourning," she sniffed.

"For whom?"

"All the beautiful children you'll never have." She sniffed. "When Katherine left, I thought you had lost every chance for happiness. I was distraught. I knew you'd never have a lovely little son to carry on the Thornecrest title."

"If you'll allow us some privacy," he told her, trying not to laugh, "I'm going to talk to Kate about that."

William waited for Pitty to blow them a kiss and leave the room before turning back to Kate. She returned the pin to its place in the box and set it on the table in front of her. "I think I'd better go," she said.

"Not until you hear what I have to say."

Kate waited, hoping against hope that he would say something that would make a difference. "Okay. You can start with why Jessica wore the pin last night."

He winced. "All right, but then we're not discussing that dreadful thing anymore. I realized yesterday that I had fallen in love with you." He tried to smile but failed. "I was such an idiot that I began to believe Pitty's superstitions about the diamond. She took the pin and sent it to Jessica to wear for one night. She suspected that I had fallen in love with you, and wanted to try it on someone else. It didn't work, of course. Which was probably her point all along. I think she wanted to prove that I was truly and deeply in love for the first time in my miserable life."

"You don't have to look so unhappy about it."

"I've wanted you from the first moment I saw you," he admitted. He touched her cheek. "It had nothing to do with the pin."

"I didn't want to fall in love with you, either."

"But you did?" He looked hopeful.

"Yes." Kate guessed it wouldn't hurt to admit it. She wondered if she had any pride left at all. "I certainly did."

"I can't tell you how relieved I am to hear that."

She twined her arms around his neck. "What are we going to do now?"

He leaned closer and brushed his lips against hers. "Well, I have several excellent suggestions. I had plenty of time to think of all sorts of things last night."

"For instance?"

"Pot roast," he said, kissing her briefly. "Apple pies." He kissed her briefly. "Children playing dress-up in the attic."

"Do you know what you're saying?"

"Of course not." He lifted his head and smiled down at her. "I'm under a spell. Will you marry me anyway?"

Kate's heart beat faster. She wondered if she'd heard correctly. "I thought you were against marriage and commitment."

"You've changed my mind," he said. "Say yes."

Kate opened her mouth, but no sound came out.

"I hoped you'd agree," he murmured, rummaging in his jacket pocket. He brought out a small velvet box and opened it. "If not, I planned to bribe you with jewels." Kate looked down as he removed an emerald-and-diamond band. Set in gold and dotted with tiny pearls, it resembled the delicate antique ring she'd seen in

Covent Garden. "It's not the same one, of course," he explained. "But I spent the morning hounding Eric at Antiquarius for something similar. Do you like it?"

"It's the most beautiful thing I've ever seen."

"Then you'll marry me?"

"Yes," she managed to say, then watched as he slipped the ring on her finger. "There's something I should warn you about."

Will stopped, his expression serious. "Whatever it is won't matter. We can visit your sisters as often as you like. And there is plenty of room at Thorne Hall for long visits. I've always envied friends with large families."

She smiled. "I think you should know that there hasn't been a boy born in our family for as long as anyone can remember."

"I'll change that," he promised with a very dukelike confidence. "We can start tonight."

"Uh-oh. How am I going to explain this to my sisters? They'll think I've lost my mind."

William wrapped her securely in his arms and bent to kiss his future duchess. He didn't care what anyone thought as long as he had Katie to share his life. "Tell them the fault belongs to Aunt Laurabelle."

Epilogue

"SHE HAS YOUR TEMPER," William noted, trying to distract eight-month-old Laura Anne Landry, who was intent on pulling his hair. He handed her a rattle, and she banged it loudly on the tray of the high chair. Sitting quietly in a high chair was not one of her favorite pastimes. She preferred to be carried around the house and the estate so she could observe everything that went on.

"He has your dignity," Kate, who held the chubby tenth Duke of Thornecrest in her lap, stated. She finished retying his left shoe before looking over at his twin sister. Little William smiled at his father, but made no move to show he was discontent with his situation. "Which may or may not be a good thing," she added, smiling at her husband.

"Fatherhood has taken away every shred of dignity I possess. Just ask Pitty." His daughter squealed for attention, so he scooted his chair closer and let her give him a hug. "See what I mean?"

"Ask Pitty what?" The elderly woman hurried into the dining room, a sheaf of papers clutched to the bodice of a fuchsia dress. Laura's eyes lit up and she banged the rattle with more gusto than usual. "Never mind. It's too exciting!" Pitty said, dropping her papers on the table. "After all this time I've finally discovered the

connection!" She beamed at Kate. "With your sisters'
assistance, of course. We've had ourselves quite a little
treasure hunt."

Will gently removed his daughter's fingers from his
hair and glanced over at his wife. She shrugged, planted
a kiss on little Willie's curly head and winked at her
husband. William melted, as he did every day at the
sight of his beautiful wife. She'd been a whirlwind of
activity since their marriage. She'd redecorated Thorne
Hall, cleaned out the attic and installed a gift shop in a
stone cottage beside the cheese factory. She'd been de-
lighted with pregnancy and motherhood, despite his
fears for her health. Her sisters and their families had
welcomed him as part of the family, and her nieces sent
him letters and colored drawings. Not an hour went by
that he didn't feel intense gratitude for the gifts he'd
been given.

"William! You're not paying attention!"

"Sorry, Pitty." He gave Kate an apologetic smile and
turned to his grandmother. "What are you trying to tell
us?"

"Good news, my dears." She took a deep breath before making her announcement. "Katherine's ancestors were not thieves after all!"

"Well, that's a relief," Will replied, trying to keep a
straight face so he wouldn't hurt the elderly woman's
feelings. "What on earth are you talking about?"

"The brooch, of course. I've finally discovered the
family connection. The diaries belonged to Alicia Landry, the third Duke of Thornecrest's daughter. It was
her clothes you found in the attic last year. She eloped
with a very unsuitable young man in 1814 and took the
brooch with her. By rights it would have been hers,
since her mother had died the year before. The Duke

was so furious he disowned her, and her husband gambled all their money away."

"Poor thing," Kate murmured. "What happened to her?"

"They left for America. He must have died at a very young age, because there are no records of him at all." She flipped through papers until she found the one she wanted. "This is where you come in, Katherine. Alicia married a cattle rancher from Montana and had three children. One of them was your great-great-grandmother."

"So the pin really belonged to me after all?"

"Yes."

"And now it belongs to Laura."

William held up his hand. "Not yet, it doesn't. Not until she's...twenty-five. Or thirty. She's staying home with her father until then."

Pitty looked thoughtful and turned to Kate. "Would you mind if I wore it in the meantime? Thorne House is quite empty now that you spend all your time in the country. I could do with a little romance myself."

"Be my guest," Kate said, struggling to hide her laughter. "Will put it back in the vault in town, and you're welcome to it."

"That's right," William echoed, reaching across the table for his wife's hand. His son grinned at him again, and his daughter whacked him on the head with her chubby fist. "But be careful. That brooch does strange things to a man."

"I've noticed." Pitty sniffed, eyeing the happy family with great satisfaction. "Which is exactly what I intended all along."